PURRFECT NAP

THE MYSTERIES OF MAX 59

NIC SAINT

PURRFECT NAP

The Mysteries of Max 59

Illustrations by Mark Beech
Edited by Chereese Graves

www.nicsaint.com

Give feedback on the book at: info@nicsaint.com

facebook.com/nicsaintauthor
@nicsaintauthor

First Edition

Printed in the U.S.A

Introduction

Introducing our fearsome foursome and their human companions.

MAX

DOOLEY

HARRIET

BRUTUS

ODELIA KINGSLEY

CHASE KINGSLEY

MARGE POOLE

TEX POOLE

UNCLE ALEC

VESTA MUFFIN

PURRFECT NAP

To Nap or Not to Nap, That is the Question

Lately me and my friends had been suffering from insomnia, which is when I suddenly remembered the existence of the so-called Master Soporific Word, a word that when uttered puts you right to sleep. The problem was that I couldn't remember the word itself, which is why I decided to take a moment and reflect. A little solititude. Some peace and quiet. Of course I should have known that the moment I removed myself from the scene, all hell would break loose. And so before long I was hot on the trail of a gang of kidnappers. At least until they started targeting me!

CHAPTER 1

"Ho-mer." Dooley looked up from the tablet computer with a frown. "Who is Ho-mer, Max?"

"I'm sure I don't know," I said. And frankly I couldn't be bothered. I was trying to perfect my napping technique, you see. It's no easy feat to enjoy the perfect nap, but I was gradually working my way up to it.

"It's something to do with Greek mythology," my friend said.

"It sounds sleep-inducing," I murmured. "Could you repeat that a couple of times? See if it does the trick."

"Ho-mer," Dooley said obligingly. "Ho-mer. Ho-mer. Ho-mer."

"Mh. No, it doesn't work," I said, shaking my head.

"What are you looking for?" asked Dooley.

"Well, I'm not sure where I heard this, but rumor has it that there is a certain phrase, or a very specific word that works as the perfect soporific, in the sense that once you hear it, you immediately fall into a deep, profound sleep. The problem is that it's a different word for every cat, though there's supposed to be a master word, a word that can put anyone to sleep, whether man or beast, and works across all the different species."

Dooley looked up. "Ho-mer," he repeated softly, but then shook his head. "I don't feel sleepy at all."

"That means it's not the right word. Once uttered it should put you to sleep within seconds—milliseconds even."

"Darn it," said Dooley, for once going to the extreme lengths of using a curse word. It just goes to show how perturbed he was.

"Let's ask Odelia," I suggested. "She's very smart. I'm sure if anyone knows who this fellow Homer is, it's her."

"All right," Dooley agreed. "We'll ask Odelia once she gets home from work." And so he placed his head on his front paws and endeavored to go to sleep. Of course sleep wouldn't come, and I could have told him why this was: he hadn't discovered the soporific word yet. And as long as he hadn't, sleep would elude him—and me, of course.

I probably should have mentioned that the four of us—Harriet and Brutus being the other members of Odelia's feline menagerie—had been having trouble sleeping for a little while now. I didn't know why this was, but it certainly was very annoying, since cats need a lot of sleep. Eighteen hours, at last count, whereas humans only need a fraction of this. But then humans are a busy breed. Always busy, busy, busy. And before you know it, they burn up. Or out. Or something along those lines. Cats rarely suffer burnout. It might happen, but I'd say it's rare. And that's because we never bite off more than we can chew. We know our strengths but also our limitations. Our strength is our capacity for napping, and until very recently my personal limitation was that I don't have a limitation. In theory I can sleep forever—taking into account the occasional bathroom and meal breaks, of course.

Harriet and Brutus now joined us. Harriet, a white Persian who invariably looks as if she just walked out of a pet salon, now appeared haggard and bleary-eyed. Even her fine white fur had lost some of its customary luster. And Brutus looked even worse: the big black cat was actually swaying on his paws, and collapsed the moment he reached us.

"This is just too much," he groaned. "I can't take much more of this, you guys. Why, oh why can't I have a decent day's sleep!"

"It's a mystery," I admitted.

"This has never happened to me before," said Harriet. "Never, ever ever. Never!" she added for good measure, making sure we got the drift. "So why is it happening to me now? Why, Max—why!!!"

"I don't know," I said. "The weird thing is that it's only happening to the four of us. As far as I can tell, none of our friends are suffering from this weird ordeal."

"It's true," said Harriet as she stretched out on the patio. "I talked to Shanille last night and she says she has no trouble sleeping. Kingman, same story. Or Buster—or any of the others."

"You have to figure this out, Max," Brutus pleaded. "I'm so tired I can't even reach my food bowl anymore! Pretty soon I'll starve to death!"

We all looked appropriately concerned. When Brutus, who's always been known for his excellent appetite, is forced to forego his daily intake of nourishment due to a general feeling of fatigue, it doesn't bode well for the rest of us.

"Max is looking for a terrific word," Dooley said. "It's a

word that will put us all to sleep in seconds. And he almost had it, but then he didn't."

"Soporific word," I corrected my friend. "Not terrific." Though if it worked that would be terrific, of course.

"What's all this nonsense about a soporific word?" Brutus grumbled. "We need answers, Max, not another one of your silly riddles!"

"It's not a silly riddle," I said. "The soporific word, and more importantly the Master Soporific Word, will put anyone to sleep when uttered, it is that powerful. Now if only I could remember. Either someone once told me, or I read about it."

"If this keeps up we'll have to ask Odelia to take us to Vena," said Harriet, shaking her head sadly. "And then where will we be?"

Vena Aleman is our local veterinarian and has cornered the market on pet harassment. The moment she sees a pet her fingers start to twitch and she frantically starts rummaging around for a needle so she can give us one of her trademark shots. Never in the annals of Hampton Cove history has a pet been known to enter Vena's lair and escape without looking like a pincushion. It's an irresistible urge with the woman. A knee-jerk reaction.

"Not Vena!" Brutus cried, understandably aghast at this suggestion from his mate.

But Harriet wasn't kidding. "I once heard Vena claim that she can put an elephant to sleep, or a lion, or any member of the circus flock. And if she can put an elephant to sleep, how hard can it be to put us to sleep?" She gave us a hopeful look, and it was a testament to our desperation that we were actually contemplating putting our fate in the hands of this known pet butcheress!

"Did she also mention if these elephants and lions and

whatnot ever wake up again after being put to sleep?" I asked.

Harriet gasped. "Oh, no!"

"Oh, yes," I said grimly. "Vena puts a lot of pets to sleep, it's what she does, but no one ever mentions the fact that they never wake up again—ever!"

"At this point I don't really care all that much about waking up again," Brutus said as he lay hugging the patio floor, his limbs pointing in the four directions of the wind. "As long as I can finally enjoy some sweet, sweet sleep!"

"You guys, did you know that sleep deprivation is actually a torture technique?" asked Dooley. "It's true," he added when Brutus gave him a dirty look—or as dirty as he could muster on an empty stomach. "You can make a person say or do anything if you keep them awake. So maybe that's what's happening here? Maybe we're all part of some psychological experiment?"

"I doubt it," I said. "Mostly they use these techniques on prisoners, trying to make them confess to some crime. But what possible crimes could we confess to? We're cats, not terrorists."

"No, that's true," Dooley admitted. "Still, maybe you should look into this, Max. Maybe someone is targeting us for some reason. Some bad person. Or some hostile foreign power." And he proceeded to give me a hopeful look.

And now that I paid attention, I saw that all three of my friends were giving me what can only be interpreted as pointed looks of utter desperation.

No pressure!

CHAPTER 2

Odelia was worried. For the past couple of days her cats had seemed out of sorts somehow. Hyper was the word her husband Chase had used last night. As if something was bothering them. She'd asked Max, of course, but he had brushed off her concerns and said everything was fine. But then why didn't they look fine?

Even Harriet, who was always so fussy about her physical appearance, looked as if she'd been in the wars. Her fur had lost its trademark shine and was even matted, something the prissy Persian would otherwise never allow. And then there was Brutus, who was even more grumpy than usual, even dispirited, which wasn't his custom.

No, something was wrong, and if Max wasn't going to admit it, out of misplaced pride or sense of discretion, she had no alternative but to take the furry foursome to the vet for a thorough examination.

Just at that moment, her boss walked into her office. Dan wore a thoughtful frown on his face, as if he was chewing on something. Right now he was chewing on his white beard, which was part of his personal style and had even made it onto the masthead of the *Hampton Cove Gazette*. A couple of years ago a cartoonist had submitted a very lifelike rendering of the Gazette's editor and Dan had liked it so much he'd struck a deal with the talented young artist and now the Gazette's logo featured the white-bearded editor, his eyes sparkling intelligently from behind round-framed glasses and his beard gently flapping in the breeze.

"What's wrong?" Odelia asked immediately. After having worked for Dan for as long as she had, she could read the man's moods like a book.

"I'm not sure," said Dan as he paced up and down her office, his hands clasped behind his back and his back ramrod straight. "Something has come to my attention and I'm not sure what to do with it, to be honest." He suddenly rounded on her. "It's you, Odelia. Or, more precisely, your relationship with the forces of law and order in this town."

"My uncle, you mean?"

"Amongst others," said Dan, nodding. "I received a phone call just now from a concerned citizen who prefers to remain anonymous, and who claims that the interests of the Gazette are too closely aligned with those of the folks who run this town. And not coincidentally three of those people happen to be related to my star reporter." He ticked them off on his fingers: "The Chief of Police, who is your uncle. The Mayor, who is your uncle's partner. And of course your husband, who is a detective with the Hampton Cove Police Department."

"Okay," said Odelia, puzzled. "So my husband is a cop, and so is my uncle. What does that have to do with anything?"

"There are those who seem to feel these connections

might cloud your judgment," said Dan as he finally took a seat. "That your independent view of things is jeopardized by these close ties."

Odelia felt a little stung by this critique. "I promise you that—"

"I know, I know," said Dan, waving his hand in a gesture of dismissal. "Personally I don't question your judgment. You're a seasoned reporter and I've never had reason to doubt your independence. But…"

"But what?" she asked, feeling thoroughly incensed by the suggestion that her close association with these so-called 'forces of law and order' would ever cloud her personal judgment.

"The person who voiced these concerns isn't alone. There have been others." He arched a meaningful and furry eyebrow. "In fact over a dozen letters have reached me in the past six months alone wondering whether the Gazette's editorial line hasn't been compromised by the presence of such a partisan voice."

"Partisan! Me!" Odelia cried.

"Look, it's not me who's saying all of these things," said Dan. "But if members of the public are voicing these concerns, they need to be addressed, wouldn't you agree? In the interest of the paper?"

Odelia, who'd been ready to launch into a long tirade defending her independence, lost some of her pep. "I guess so," she finally admitted. "But how are we supposed to 'address' these concerns, Dan? I can't go and divorce my husband, now can I? Or stop speaking to my uncle or his girlfriend?"

"Of course not. And frankly I wouldn't change a thing about who you are or what you do. Your close association with the police force has served this paper well in the past, leading us to publish the kinds of scoops other papers can only dream of. But maybe…" He hesitated, eyeing her very closely all of a sudden.

"Maybe what?" she asked, afraid of what he was about to say.

"Maybe we should… diversify. You know, add a few more people to the roster. People who can't be accused of towing the Town Hall line—or having any kind of connection to the local constabulary."

"You mean hire more reporters? But I thought you said you didn't have the budget?"

"Oh, I don't," said Dan, a cunning little smile now spreading across his wizened features. "But there's plenty of people who would love nothing better than to contribute to the Gazette—gratis."

She stared at the man. Dan's eyes were glittering, and for a moment she wondered if he had finally lost his marbles. "You want to hire a fresh batch of reporters and not pay them?"

"Exactly!" said Dan, pointing at her like a game show host whose candidate has just guessed the answer to the million-dollar question.

"I'm afraid I don't—"

"Of course you don't! And neither did I, until this morning, when I scanned through the online comments on our Facebook page. Reams and reams of comments, I might add. Big chunks of text. All supplied to us free of charge by those eager-beaver internauts—bless their little hearts."

Odelia still didn't see where Dan was going with this. All she knew was that she didn't like it. First being accused of being partisan, and now her position was being jeopardized by reporters willing to work sans remuneration.

Who was to say that she, too, wouldn't be working gratis very soon now?

"Don't you see?" said Dan, when he detected a marked lack of excitement in his one and only employee.

"Not really," she had to admit.

"Volunteers!" Dan cried jubilantly. "We simply ask our loyal army of online fans to turn their screeds into copy and we're set!"

"But these people aren't reporters, Dan," she felt obliged to point out. "They're regular people. Housewives, plumbers, carpenters, truck drivers, students..."

"So? We'll call it the democratization of the *Hampton Cove Gazette*. From now on anyone who can string two sentences together can participate. Let's see them complain about our lack of independence then! Ha!"

Odelia blinked a few times. "So... you're going to publish pieces from anyone who can hold a pen?"

"Not a pen, honey," said Dan. "A phone! A keyboard! A tablet! It's new media meeting old media. And it's going to give us a much-needed kick in the rear. Revolutionize the way we do things. We've become stale. Complacent. But no more!"

"Mh," she said, not fully convinced but not willing to voice her reservations for fear of being given the pink slip. As it stood, she might be made redundant anyway, if these internauts, these social media warriors, were going to provide the bulk of the content for the Gazette from now on. Why pay her a handsome salary if Dan could source some prime content without having to pay a dime?

"Look, let's just give it a shot, okay?" said the editor as he got up. "But I have to tell you that I have a great feeling about this." And he gave her two thumbs up to express just how great this feeling was.

She gave him a feeble smile and her own slightly less

exuberant version of the same gesture. "Let's do this," she said finally.

And as he left her office, she had the sinking feeling one gets when imminent unemployment is staring them in the face.

CHAPTER 3

Tex had been scraping some sticky substance from Norbert, his number-one gnome—the big bearded one who stood sentinel near the dividing hedge with his neighbor Ted Trapper—when he got up out of his crouched position to wipe his sweaty brow. He didn't know who had placed the sticky substance on the pride of his collection but whoever it was, he would make darn sure it would never happen again. As far as he could tell it was a piece of gum, and since it had been placed across Norbert's visage, it had proven exceedingly difficult to get off, especially from the poor gnome's eyes, mouth and nose —and beard of course.

And it wasn't the first time either. Last week one of his minor gnomes, Jackson Brown, had been the unfortunate victim of a similar attack, an act of vandalism so heinous and appalling it had brought tears to the good doctor's eyes. For in Jackson Brown's case it wasn't muck to the mug but a whack to the nose, lopping the appendage clear off. Tex had searched high and low for the poor thing's nose so he could reattach it with superglue but the culprits must have taken it along with them as a souvenir—a token of the heinousness of their crime.

Marge came walking out of the house with a load of wash under her arm and stopped to see what her husband was doing. "Why don't you use a steel wire brush, honey?" she suggested.

"A steel wire brush!" he cried, indignation making him raise his voice to a squeak. "That'll destroy Norbert's whole face! Remove all of the paint!"

"So? You can paint his face back on later. But then at least you won't spend the rest of the day trying to get that yucky stuff off of him."

"This here gnome is a work of art," he grumbled, gesticulating at the treasured item. "You don't take a steel brush to a Picasso or a Monet, do you? Or to the Mona Lisa, while you're at it?"

"If I remember correctly you got this particular gnome at Costco, honey," said Marge dryly, and walked on.

He gave her retreating back a dirty look.

"I saw that!" she said.

"Oh, rats," he muttered.

At least she hadn't told him to ditch the gnome and buy a new one—three for the price of two this week in Costco's Fall Sale.

"Trouble in paradise, Tex?" suddenly a voice rang out.

He immediately recognized it as belonging to Ted Trapper.

"Nothing I can't handle," he replied, blocking his neighbor's sight of Norbert's damaged features. Ted was something of a gnome aficionado himself, and for a long time a friendly rivalry had existed between the two gnome collectors.

"I saw someone took a big whack at Jackson Brown's nose last week?" Ted said, sounding far too cheerful for

Tex's liking. "And that chewing gum they put on Norbert must be hard to get off."

Tex gave his neighbor a not-too-friendly look. "You wouldn't happen to know the person responsible, would you, Ted?" he said, and if there was an implication that he suspected Ted of being behind both acts of vandalism it was because the man was his number-one suspect.

Ted's face took on that holier-than-thou expression Tex detested so much. "Who, me? Oh, no, neighbor. If I had seen who took a spade to Jackson Brown and stuck a big ol' piece of gum on Norbert I'd have already told you. In fact I would personally have filed a complaint with the police against the miscreant—yes, sir. It doesn't do for vandals to wander around our peaceful neighborhood and defile our personal property—it doesn't do at all. Nuh-uh."

"A spade, huh? And why would you say they used a spade?"

"Just speculating, Tex. Considering the damage a spade seems likely."

"You would use a spade, would you?"

"I would use a spade," Ted confirmed.

"So *did* you use a spade?" he demanded.

Ted gave him an injured look. "I would never touch a gnome in anger, Tex. I love the little fellas far too much to stoop to such objectionable behavior."

"It's odd, though, isn't it, Ted?" said Tex, approaching the hedge above which his neighbor's bespectacled head was peeping.

"What is, Tex?" asked Ted innocently as he pushed his glasses further up his nose.

"That while two of my gnomes were attacked in the space of less than a week, none of yours were. Even though your collection is easily as big as mine."

"But nowhere near as nice," Ted hastened to state in a

sickening attempt at flattery. "Nowhere near as nice as yours, Tex."

"Be that as it may," said Tex, who might see through this obvious ruse but still felt himself softening toward his next-door neighbor. He was only human, after all, and as such not immune to praise, whether coming from a brown-nosing gnome-destroying vandal or not. "Your collection is only a hop and a skip across the hedge away, and yet none of your precious gnomes were harmed—not a single one. And so I can't help wondering why." He directed a look of abject suspicion at his immediate competitor, a look Ted took in his stride, if the smirk that now rose up his cherubic features was any indication.

"I guess they didn't think my collection was worth defiling, Tex," the accountant stated with a little shrug. "After all, it wasn't my top gnome that was featured on the front page of the Gazette last month, clutched in the arms of its proud owner. And it wasn't my daughter who wrote a puff piece about her father's favorite hobby."

"It wasn't a puff piece," Tex snapped. "She simply gave her unbiased opinion, just like she does in all of her interviews."

"I'm just saying, neighbor," said Ted. "All of that attention comes at a price. It attracts the wrong kind of people —the vandalic kind."

It could be Tex's imagination, but a strange gleam seemed to have come into Ted's eyes. The gleam of a man who sees justice done.

"Anyhoo," said Ted, giving the hedge a light tap across the top. "Gotta run, Tex. Duty calls. But I do hope you get Jackson Brown's nose fixed and Norbert's face cleaned. It does detract from their value—by a lot, I would guess. And they aren't insured, or so your wife tells me. And with the big contest coming up..."

He left Tex fuming and grinding his teeth at such insolence. But he couldn't exactly come out and accuse Ted of being the mastermind behind this monstrous case of hooliganism now could he? Not without evidence to back him up. Ted was right, though. He needed Norbert and Jackson Brown in tip-top shape for the Gnome of the Year competition. The jury might deduct points if they detected a shoddy repair job on either of his top contenders.

Which brought him right back to his original idea: to install a security system in his backyard. Protect his personal property the way it should be protected: by a state-of-the-art array of cameras. And as he contemplated the ins and outs of his plan, he returned to the tedious task of painstakingly removing gum from his gnome.

CHAPTER 4

Johnny Carew watched the progress Tex Poole made with his gnome with distinct interest.

"Why goes Tex keep rubbing that gnome's head, Jer?" he asked. "Does he think a genie will appear and grant him three wishes?"

"Will you shut up for one second," his friend grunted. "I'm trying to think here."

Both men were ensconced in the plot of land that lines the Poole backyard, with Johnny keeping a close eye on all the goings-on while his friend Jerry Vale was currently wrestling with a most difficult proposition. For the longest time Johnny and Jerry had been career crooks, and had probably spent more time in the slammer than enjoying their freedom. But ever since returning from Mexico after their latest stunt, and having done their time, they had decided to take another stab at walking the straight and narrow.

And yet they were currently holed up in a field spying on the residents of Harrington Street.

"He looks angry," Johnny remarked. "Someone must

have sold him the wrong gnome, Jer. A gnome without a genie inside."

"Genies don't exist, you moron," said Jerry. "And if they did exist, they sure as heck wouldn't go hiding in any cheap plaster gnomes."

"Would be nice if they did, though, wouldn't it?" said Johnny with a dreamy look in his mellow brown eyes. "Imagine being able to rub a gnome and having all your wishes come true. What would you wish, Jer, if you could rub a gnome?"

"I'd wish for a partner who knew when to shut up."

But Johnny wasn't perturbed in the least by this outburst, and that dreamy look didn't diminish by a single flicker. "I'd wish for horses," he said now.

In spite of his admonition that he was so busy he couldn't be disturbed, Jerry looked up at this. "Horses? What do you need horses for, you dummy?"

Johnny pulled his huge shoulders up to his sizable ears. "I don't know. I always wanted to do something with horses. On a farm, maybe. A horse farm, you know," he clarified, in case it wasn't obvious. "That's a farm where they keep horses."

"For me it's pigs," said Jer, a slight smile playing about his lips. It lit up his ferrety face and made him look almost human. "Ever since I was a little scrapper I dreamed of raising pigs. Nice big fat porkers. Don't ask me why. It's just something I thought would be cool." But then he snapped out of this roseate dream of porkers. "Will you shut up about horses and pigs and let me focus!"

"You're the one who mentioned pigs, Jer," Johnny said.

"Whatever," Jerry muttered, and got on with the complicated task of connecting the wireless camera he had attached to the fence to the app on his laptop. "There," he said with a touch of satisfaction when a clear image appeared. "That should do it."

Johnny glanced at the laptop. "Hey, that's Tex. How did he get in your laptop?"

"He didn't get in my laptop," said Jerry as he rubbed his hands with glee. "But this here footage sure did." He gave his partner a grin. "Looks like we're in business, buddy!"

"Oh, goodie," said Johnny, even though he had absolutely no clue what his friend and business partner was going on about. All he could think was that Jerry had never looked more like a ferret than he did at that moment. A happy ferret, sure, but still a ferret.

* * *

EDGAR COOPER—ED to his friends—had been walking the streets of Hampton Cove for several days now, and he had the impression he was finally getting the hang of this town. When he first arrived he'd been surprised at how big the place was, contrary to the comments he'd read on TripAdvisor and heard from some of his friends who'd recommended this 'coastal jewel in the Hamptons crown' as they called it. Mostly he'd spent his mornings on the beach, his afternoons combing through some of the little shops and museums the town boasted, and then in the late afternoon, when the sun had ceased to give so much of its heat, back to the beach. His nights, of course, had been spent frequenting the many restaurants and eateries.

In other words: his was the perfect tourist life. But even though he should have been having a blast, one minor point detracted from the perfect holiday experience: his fiancée who had stood him up on the morning of the big day. This was supposed to be their honeymoon, and frankly a honeymoon with only the groom and not the bride wasn't much of a honeymoon at all, now was it?

At first Ed wanted to cancel this trip, being thoroughly discombobulated by Sara's change of heart, but then his mom had convinced him that since the hotel had been paid for, he might as well make the most of it—and so he had. To some extent. He still suffered from the occasional emotional outburst from time to time, remembering Sara's text message announcing that the wedding was off. Since the text message had arrived when he was standing in front of the altar, with the officiating priest impatiently looking at his watch and a church full of friends and family becoming antsy, it was a moment that was etched in his memory—and probably would be forevermore and then some.

And since he hadn't been able to face the congregation and announce that the wedding was off, he'd handed his cell phone to his mom and had fled the scene, leaving the hard task of breaking the bad news to that indomitable woman.

He arrived back at the Star Hotel, located in the heart of town, and approached the desk. "Any messages?" he asked, even though by all rights he should have known that Sara, if she had another change of heart, would send him a text.

The receptionist's shake of the head told him everything he needed to know, and so he turned on his heel and headed for the elevator.

Arriving on the third floor, he opened the door of the modest room with his key card and stepped inside. The room was all he'd been able to afford on his meager salary. He worked as a customer service agent at a debt collection agency, and even though business was booming, even as the economy was tanking, or perhaps because of it, his salary lacked the oomph to book the bridal suite. Maybe that's why Sara had broken off the wedding? Because he was poor?

"Mom," he called out when he couldn't immediately locate his progenitor. "Have you been talking to the staff again? I couldn't help but notice that the receptionist was looking at me as if I was a drowning victim that needs saving." When no answer was forthcoming, he walked out onto the balcony, and found the ancestor taking in some sun whilst selecting a petit four from a tray. "You do realize I'm getting billed for those, don't you?" he asked as he took a seat.

"Oh, you know as well as I do that everything was paid for in advance," she said as she popped something small and pink into her mouth and closed her eyes with relish. "Mh... You should try one of these, Ed. They're to die for."

"If you eat that entire tray you will die," he told her morosely as he slumped in his chair. "It's full of sugar, saturated fats and probably a lot of other junk."

"Oh, stop being such a grouch and try one," she said, and tried to aim one of the little delights into his mouth.

He expertly dodged her motherly hand and said, "I'm not kidding, Mom. This stuff isn't good for you."

"Spoilsport," she said, and bit down on the treat herself. "For once in your life put on your party hat," she suggested as she lay back in her chair. For the occasion she was donning a bathing suit that accentuated her curvy features. When people saw the two of them together they couldn't believe they were related. Whereas Ed was tall and gangly, his mother was short and round. And whereas he was bald, she had a thick mane of curly blond hair.

"You shouldn't go around telling absolute strangers about my personal misfortune, Mom," he said as he rubbed his eyes.

"But they already know, Ed!" she said. "They read your name and they know that you're that guy."

"So what if I don't want to be 'that' guy?"

"Tough luck. You shouldn't have told cousin Danny to film the wedding. You should have known he would put the whole thing on BooToob."

"YouTube."

"One million views, sweetheart. We're famous!"

"I'm famous, you mean." Or rather, infamous.

Cousin Danny, whatever his faults, had certainly picked his moment. Exactly when Ed had read Sara's message and his face had crumpled like a used tissue, Danny had zoomed in on him, capturing his distress in all its dubious glory. The subsequent handing over of the phone and the race from the altar, then Mom reading out Sara's terse text in front of the whole church, and then of course Uncle Frank grabbing a nearby bouquet of pink peonies and hitting Sara's dad over the head with it and the resulting brawl had quickly gone viral.

"Danny told me Hollywood is interested," said Mom. "They want to turn it into a romantic comedy featuring Mandy Moore."

"Oh, God," he muttered as he hung his head.

"And guess who's playing you?"

"I don't want to know."

"Channing Tatum!"

"Sara doesn't look anything like Mandy Moore," he told her.

"She does a little. And of course you're the spitting image of Channing Tatum, sweetheart. Though I hope they won't make him shave off that wonderful head of hair of his. That would be such a shame. And you never know if it'll grow back as nice as before."

Not for the first time since Mom had talked him into

going on this honeymoon with her he thoroughly regretted his decision. In his defense he'd been weak and downhearted and hadn't put up much of a fight when she suggested it. Her arguments had sounded good, too: the money had already been spent, and unfortunately he hadn't had the foresight to get cancellation insurance—what honeymooner does? So why not go and take advantage of the trip and add Mom to the roster? Sara's loss was Mom's gain. Or as Mom put it: she might have lost a daughter-in-law but at least she got to visit the Hamptons, something she'd been wanting to do for a long time. 'It's on my sucker list!' she had told him.

He noticed how his mother was giving him a critical look and he knew that another speech was forthcoming. Ever since they'd embarked on this journey she'd been trying to get the message across that maybe the fact that Sara had left him at the altar wasn't such a bad thing. After all, better she had that change of heart before tying the knot and linking her fate to his than after. Right?

"You'll meet someone new," Mom was saying now, another variation on the same theme. "Just you wait and see. You and Sara weren't meant to be, Ed. Trust me: it's better this way."

"Yes, Mom," he said, and sighed deeply. "Of course it is."

CHAPTER 5

To be absolutely honest it wasn't so much the fact that I couldn't sleep that was worrying me but the consequences of this lack of sleep. Dooley had convinced me that after a period of not getting sufficient repose the mental faculties start being affected and the victim of insomnia might even start hallucinating and go stark-raving mad!

My friends sometimes praise me for being in the possession of a big brain, and even though I don't agree with this assessment, it is true that I have a certain facility for coming up with original solutions to problems that might vex a lesser feline. Case in point: our human Odelia, who works as a reporter for the *Hampton Cove Gazette*, comes across the odd mystery from time to time, and rather than allowing this to baffle me, like it often does her and her husband Chase, I work through the clues and have often been instrumental in the identification and subsequent arrest of the culprit.

And now it would appear I was on the verge of losing

this 'knack' as you might call it—all because I couldn't sleep!

"We have to figure out what this Terrific Word is, Max," Dooley said, piling on the pressure. "Or else we're all toast —all of us!" He gave me a look of intense concern. "Though especially you, Max. That big, beautiful brain of yours might not survive."

"It's a Soporific Word, not a Terrific Word," I murmured as I gave myself up to thought. If my friend was correct—and I had no reason to assume that he wasn't—pretty soon my brain would get all scrambly and screwy and start to shrivel and shrink to the size of a raisin, so I had to make use of it while I still could!

"It must be something in the food," Brutus opined.

"It could be something in the water," Harriet offered.

"It might be something in the air," Dooley suggested.

"Will you guys let me think for a moment?" I said with some heat. I mean, really. How is a cat supposed to come up with the solution to a life-threatening problem if people keep yapping away? And with people I mean cats, of course.

"Whatever it is, it's certainly making you cranky," said Harriet, looking hurt at my outburst.

"Yeah, we're only trying to help, Maxie baby," said Brutus as he suppressed a yawn. "Throwing some suggestions out there, you know. Brainstorm the issue in this focus group we've got going here."

"I don't need a focus group. All I need is some peace and quiet so I can think," I told my friends. "Is that so much to ask?"

"Touchy," Harriet said as she raised a critical eyebrow.

"Very," Brutus agreed as he gave me a curious look.

Coming from one usually as meek as myself, he was probably surprised by all the backtalk.

"Max is tired," Dooley said. "Lack of sleep has that effect, you know. It makes you irritable. In fact it's the final stage before the patient loses grip on reality and starts seeing things." He eyed me closely for a moment, then held up his paw. "How many paws am I holding up, Max?"

"Five," I said, and smiled at his sharp intake of breath. "One, silly. I'm not losing my marbles just yet."

"Oh, thank God!" said Dooley. "I thought you'd lost it!"

"At least Max still has his sense of humor," said Harriet.

"If you can call that kind of wisecrack humor," Brutus added.

"It's true that Max doesn't have a funny bone in his body," Harriet remarked. "He might be clever, but he's not very funny."

"Not only is he not funny, he's also very boring," said Brutus. "I only have to listen to him talk and I start nodding off. Except now. Now I'm wide awake."

"I'm right here, you guys," I pointed out. Though still not any closer to finding out the reason the four of us couldn't find sleep.

"Look, maybe we should leave Max in peace," Harriet suggested. "So he can figure things out. Meanwhile we can go see a man about a dog."

"What man?" asked Dooley, immediately interested by this curious statement. "And what dog?"

"It's just an expression, Dooley," said Harriet. "Now come along, you two. Let's leave Max to exercise that big brain of his."

"That very big brain," said Brutus with a grin, "in that very big head, carried by that very thick neck and that very big body."

"Yes, yes, yes," I said, and shooed them all off so I could think. I'd been trying to remember where I'd heard that story about the Master Soporific Word, but for the life of me the solution wouldn't come. But you know what they say: when you can't remember something, rather than rack your brain, you should go and do something completely different—preferably some physical activity that isn't too strenuous, like gardening or doing the dishes. Before long the answer will pop into your head. Now I'm not big on either gardening or doing the dishes, but I do enjoy going for long walks, so I decided to do just that. And so I got up from my tush, left the backyard via the rose bushes located at the bottom of the garden, and soon found myself in the field that lines the back of Odelia and her parents' property—in fact most of the properties on Harrington Street.

The field belongs to a man named Blake Carrington, who is a very rich man—one of the wealthiest in Hampton Cove, in fact. He probably could be even richer if he developed the field and built another row of family homes. But I guess he's rich enough and doesn't need the money. Also, the field is where his son died some years ago, and he likes to keep it the way it is out of respect for his boy.

And so I soon found myself pottering along, trying not to think too hard and in fact forget about my predicament, when the sound of voices reached my well-trained ears. They were the voices of two men I knew well: Johnny Carew and Jerry Vale, two career criminals who had seen the error of their ways and had decided to walk the straight and narrow from now on. Though their interpretation of what exactly constitutes the straight and narrow might be up for debate, since they had strayed from the path on more than one occasion in the recent past.

Curiosity soon held me in its grip, and so I stealthily drew closer to find out what these two were up to.

"Don't hold it like that—you're going to drop it," Jerry was saying.

"But that's how the boss told me to hold it," Johnny returned.

"And I'm telling you different. Now give me that thing."

Until that moment I'd only had sound but no picture, but that was about to change as our paths converged. The item of contention seemed to be a camera, and for some reason it was pointed straight into Tex and Marge's backyard.

"This is how you do it," said Jerry with satisfaction as he attached the small device to a minor hole in the fence. "See? It won't budge."

"You're so clever, Jer," said Johnny, his voice dripping with admiration. "I don't know what I'd do without you."

"Just hand me the next one," Jerry said, though judging from the slight smile that had slid up his face the compliment was appreciated.

I saw now that a box filled with miniature cameras stood at the men's feet, and as I looked a little closer I saw that several of them had already been attached to that selfsame fence.

And then it hit me: these two fellas were spying on my humans!

"How many more, Jer?" asked Johnny.

"How many more are there?" said Jerry as he fixed another camera in place, his tongue sticking out of his mouth as he focused on his task.

Johnny studied the box and its contents more closely. "Um, lemme see. One, two, three, four…"

"All right, all right," said Jerry with a touch of irritation. "Just give me a ballpark number, will you? A dozen? Two?"

"A dozen sounds about right," said Johnny after a pause. He scratched his sizable bulk. "Not an even dozen, though, Jer. There could be more, or there could be less."

"It doesn't matter," said Jerry as he studied his work

with a little grunt of approval. "If we don't get them done today we'll do the rest tomorrow. At any rate, the boss will be pleased."

"Let's hope so," said Johnny.

I frowned as I wondered who this boss might be. Probably some criminal mastermind who was out to rob the neighborhood. Or why else would he have his associates place surveillance cameras on the Poole home?

And as I watched, the two crooks moved onto the next backyard: my very own!

There were no two ways about it. I had to warn Odelia that she was about to be robbed. And not only she but probably the whole street, judging from the number of cameras these two were installing on this mysterious boss person's instigation.

And I was just about to abscond from the scene when something fluttery and colorful landed on my nose and I sneezed, giving my position away for sure!

The fluttery and colorful thing turned out to be a butterfly. My sneeze had caused it to depart from its perch on my nose quite speedily and with due haste, and I now found it sitting on a nearby tree branch, studying me with unveiled interest.

"Did you hear that, Jer?" said Johnny, who was glancing around in search of the source of the sound of my sneeze.

"Hear what?" said Jer, pointing one of his little gizmos at my very own home and doing a good job at it, too, judging from his grin of gratification.

"I thought I heard someone sneezing," said Johnny.

"Must be your imagination," said his friend. "There's no one here."

"If you say so," said Johnny with a shrug, taking his partner's word at face value. He was checking something on his phone, and it took me a while to realize he was looking at the footage of the camera Jerry was installing. "Looking good, Jer," he said, giving the other man two thumbs up and dropping his phone in the process.

"We haven't been formally introduced yet, have we?" the butterfly now piped up. "My name is Flora. What is yours?"

"Max," I said curtly. The fluttery little thing had almost given my position away, and since I was essentially in spy mode I wasn't exactly in a talkative mood.

"So do you live around here, Max?" asked Flora conversationally.

"Look, I can't really talk right now," I said.

"I've seen you around, you know," said Flora, ignoring my comment. "You and that fluffy little friend of yours. You live in that house over there? The one with the kid and the cute couple?"

"Yeah, that's the one," I confirmed, and made to leave the scene so I could tell Odelia to catch these two crooks in the act.

"That's a great-looking place you got there, Max," said Flora, who seemed oblivious to my desire to leave the scene post-haste. "You lead quite an interesting life, don't you? You and your friend?"

"Friends," I couldn't resist correcting her. "There's four of us."

"Oh, that's right. A big black cat and a huffy white Persian."

In spite of my desire to retreat I couldn't help but smile at this description of Harriet. "She is a little huffy, isn't she?" I admitted.

"Quite," Flora said as she flapped her colorful gossamer wings. "Only last week I was flying past her when she objected to my close proximity. Claimed I was going to soil her precious fur." She rolled her eyes. "As if! I have my pride, you know, Max, and I can tell you right now that butterflies are among the cleanest species on God's green earth. Far be it from me to cast aspersions, but your Harriet is not a nice cat."

"She's not exactly *my* Harriet," I said.

"But she is your friend—you said so yourself."

"She is my friend," I admitted.

"Then you should tell her to be a little nicer to other creatures—creatures that wish her no harm and who are simply going about their business and have no interest in spoiling anyone's precious white fur."

"I'll tell her," I promised the talkative butterfly.

"Mind that you do," said Flora. "Do you know that she actually tried to strike me with her paw? And when I proved too fast for her, she told that big black cat to catch me and he actually went and did just that? The nerve of those two!"

"Brutus caught you?" I asked with a touch of concern.

"Well, he certainly tried, but I proved too fast for him, didn't I?" she said, a distinct note of pride in her voice. "No one can catch Flora when she's going well. Everyone knows that. I'm the fastest butterfly around—faster even than Sidonia, and she's won plenty of trophies."

"Who is..."

"Sidonia? Well, she's retired now, of course, but back in the day she was quite the champ. Won every butterfly race she entered."

"I didn't know butterflies organized races," I said, much surprised. If only Dooley had been there. He would have found this conversation fascinating.

"Oh, we do," said Flora. "We like to race from flower to flower, and the one who gets there first wins first prize."

"And first prize is..."

"Why, all the nectar you can feed on, silly!" she said, as

if it was the most obvious thing in the world, which probably for her it was. A faraway look had come into her eyes at the mention of the word 'nectar.' "Yesterday I won the Race of the Roses, and I drank so much nectar I almost passed out. I might have overdone it," she said with a touch of embarrassment. "When I got home I got a good scolding for being too greedy for my own good." She shrugged. "I can't help it. I guess I was born with a competitive streak."

"Well, it was nice chatting with you, Flora," I said.

"Yeah, it was nice chatting with you, too," said Flora as she fluttered her wings by way of saying goodbye. "And please teach your friends a lesson in civility, will you? It doesn't hurt to be nice to one another."

She obviously had a lot more to say, but I told her I had to run, and so I did. I wanted Odelia or Chase to catch these crooks in the act!

CHAPTER 6

The trouble with humans is that they're never there when you need them. Since it was the middle of the day, Odelia was at work, and so were Chase and the others. In fact the only ones who were home were my friends, and it wasn't as if they were much use to me at that moment.

I arrived to find them stretched out on the lawn in Odelia's backyard. At first when I approached I thought they were asleep, but when Harriet said, "And? Has your walk stirred your memory, Max?"

"Have you remembered your Terrific Word?" Dooley asked hopefully.

"Please tell me you did," Brutus pleaded. "I need sleep, buddy, and I need it now!"

I'd totally forgotten about this insomnia issue that had been plaguing us, to be honest, since we now had bigger fish to fry. "Johnny and Jerry are spying on us," I said, launching into my story without preamble. "In fact they're spying on everyone. We have to tell someone, you guys, and catch them in the act."

"Who is spying on who?" asked Dooley, too tired to lift his head from his paws.

"Whom," Harriet corrected him. "Spying on whom."

"Who is Whom?" asked Dooley. "And who is spying on him?"

"Oh, forget it," Harriet muttered, not in the mood to explain the finer points of grammar to our young friend.

"Okay, so why are Jerry and Johnny spying on us?" asked Brutus. "We're just a couple of cats."

"They're not actually spying on us," I said, "but more on the residents who live on Harrington Street. They're installing dozens of cameras for a person they call 'the boss,' probably some well-known local crime kingpin."

"Oh, my," said Harriet with a yawn. "Imagine that."

"What is a kingpin?" asked Dooley. "Is it, like, the king of pins?"

"Yeah, Dooley," said Brutus with a grin. "The kingpin is the pin that rules all pins."

"It's a person," said Harriet. "A very important person. In this case a very important criminal person. Like a crime boss. A big bad crime boss."

"I don't like crime bosses," said Dooley. "They're not very nice."

"Nobody likes crime bosses," said Brutus. "Not even other crime bosses."

The lack of interest my story was engendering was shocking. At least it shocked me. "You guys—we have to do something!" I urged them. "These people are up to no good. They're probably out to burgle us."

"Not much to burgle," Harriet said with a chuckle.

"Yeah, Max," said Brutus. "What are they going to steal? Our kibble?"

I have to say I was seriously losing my patience. "When

I say 'us' I mean our humans. They're going to burgle our humans and we have to stop them!"

"You stop them," said Harriet with another yawn. "I'm too tired."

"Yeah, frankly I don't have the strength to stop anyone," Brutus added.

"I'll stop them," Dooley suggested. "Where is this Whom person, Max? And this Kingpin person? Or are they one and the same?"

"Gah," I said, and turned on my heel and strode off. It was no good. By the time I'd reached Odelia and she'd returned to see what was going on, Johnny and Jerry would be long gone. And so I did what no cat should ever be forced to do: I went in search of our canine neighbors.

Fifi is a Yorkshire terrier, and might not look like much, but she can be fierce when provoked. And Rufus is the sweetest dog on the planet but he's a sheepdog and looks like a woolly mammoth. And so my plan was to scare the living daylights out of the criminal twosome intent on robbing our humans blind by having Fifi dig deep and bring out her inner fighting machine, then pin them down with the assistance of Rufus.

"Max! Where are you going!"

It was Dooley, who had followed me while I pursued my mission. Harriet and Brutus, meanwhile, decided to stay put and hug the lawn, possibly in the hopes of being visited by the sandman.

"I need to stop these criminals, Dooley," I said.

"You mean this kingpin person? I'll help you, Max. We'll stop him together," he said as he fell into step next to me. He had a sort of determined look in his eyes, and it was exactly that look I'd been looking for, if you see what I mean.

I gave him a grateful smile. "Thanks, buddy. Look, what

you're about to witness is going to be tough. In fact it's almost intolerable for any right-minded feline to have to ask a *dog* for their assistance, but it simply has to be done."

He shivered violently. But then he closed his eyes and nodded. "What will be, will be," he said, echoing the words of that great philosopher Doris Day. And when he opened his eyes again, I could see the light of resolve burning bright.

"Let's do this," I said, and swallowed once or twice.

We found Fifi and Rufus gathered in the Trapper backyard. The two are great friends, and often shoot the breeze. They're a funny duo to look at: Fifi just a tiny little thing and Rufus a big, hairy bruiser. When we approached, the conversation halted and they regarded us with unveiled curiosity. "You two look serious," Rufus remarked.

"That's because we have serious business to discuss," I said.

"What business? And how serious?" asked Fifi, plunking down on her tush, her tail wagging excitedly. Dogs love it when they're being asked to go on a secret mission, even when it's cats doing the asking. Or, more accurately, especially when it's cats doing the asking. It provides spice to an otherwise dull life.

Now before you go accusing me of un-catlike behavior and betraying the cat code, let me reiterate that our humans were all at work, and so there literally wasn't anyone else we could ask. And I know that cats asking dogs to help them out is not done. In fact it's against everything I believe in. But at this juncture I had no other option. And so I forged ahead on this most distasteful task.

"We need your help," I said quietly, having trouble getting the words out.

"What was that?" asked Rufus. "Did I just hear you say you need our help, Max?" He directed a curious look at his friend, who sat looking a little stunned by this unexpected denouement.

"Cats asking dogs for help?" said Fifi as a distinct grin lit up her furry little face. "Am I hearing you right, Max? Is that what you just said?"

"Look, this isn't easy for me," I said. "So don't make me repeat it."

"Okay, fine," said Rufus. "Just tell us what you need."

"Can I do the honors?" Dooley said. When I gave him the nod, he proceeded, "There's this person called Whom and this other person called Kingpin, and they're planning to rob us blind. Though it could also be the same person. There's also two other men called Johnny and Jerry, though I don't know how they are involved, exactly. So if I'm correct there are four men, or maybe even five, and all of them are up to no good, and we have to stop them—or better yet you have to, because you're dogs, and people are scared of dogs. Or at least bad people are."

Fifi and Rufus had listened attentively. They now blinked once and turned to me, hoping for some clarification. And so I did the honors. "In actual fact the people planning to rob our humans are Johnny Carew and Jerry Vale," I said. "And they're right behind us in that field over there planting cameras so they can spy on us. I don't know who they're working for, but it must be some criminal mastermind."

"Does this have something to do with Tex's gnomes being vandalized?" asked Rufus. "I heard him practically accuse Ted this morning of being behind the vandalism."

It was the first I'd heard about Tex's gnomes being attacked, but I couldn't very well admit that I didn't know what was happening in my own backyard, now could I? So I nodded solemnly. "It might very well have something to do with the gnome incident, yes."

"Oh, my God!" said Rufus. "I bet Ted's gnomes are next!"

"Or Kurt's gnomes!" Fifi added, looking thoroughly shocked by this piece of news.

"Wait, Kurt has gnomes?" I asked. Kurt Mayfield is Fifi's human and also Odelia's next-door neighbor.

"It's a recent thing," said Fifi. "He must have seen Tex and Ted's gnomes and decided to get in on the action and get some of his own."

"It's a real plague," Rufus lamented. "Did you know that Ted actually prefers his gnomes over me?"

"No!" said Fifi in a low voice. "Really?"

Rufus nodded seriously. "Last week I really had to tinkle and I couldn't wait for Ted to take me to the dog park so I did my business in the backyard. Against Ted's biggest gnome. The one he calls Robert Parker." He seemed a little shamefaced as he relayed the story. "He's just so robust and sturdy-looking and I simply couldn't resist. And I'd just finished when a terrible ruckus broke out. There was pounding on the kitchen window and then a berserk Ted came stomping out of the house. He'd seen me relieving myself against Robert Parker and he was furious! He dragged his favorite gnome from his perch and started hosing him down with the garden hose, and I could tell from the gleam in his eye he would have liked to put that hose on me, too! Only Marcie was there, and she doesn't believe in corporal punishment, so I was saved from the ordeal."

"My God," said Fifi, shaking her head in abhorrence. "The depths of depravity humans can sink to. Putting a hose on their precious pet just because they heed nature's call. I mean, those gnomes are *made* to be used as a public lavatory."

We all studied Ted's collection of gnomes, and I had to

say there was something in what Fifi was saying. The vacuous expression on their jolly faces. Those weird pointy hats. That long white beard. They seemed to call out to our bladders to void themselves against their person. Then again, cats aren't dogs. We don't tinkle against solid immovable objects. We like to do our business in a clean environment, not where every Tom, Dick and Harry has gone before. But then that's dogs for you. They're so territorial when it comes to the art of the tinkle.

"Look, even though it's great chatting," I said, "can I reiterate that there are two crooks planning a burglarious campaign of epic proportion as we speak? And that if we want to catch them time is of the essence?"

"You're right, Max," said Rufus. "Let's go and catch these guys."

And so we left to catch us some crooks. And as we set out on our journey, I explained the battle plan I'd drawn up and the roles assigned to each member of our posse. They readily agreed, even though Fifi had some doubts about her capacity to project menace. When I told her all she had to do was bare her teeth and growl and look mean, and she gave us a quick demonstration and we told her she looked like a miniature Cujo, I think her qualms were allayed.

"I was actually scared there for a moment," Dooley told her, causing her to glow with righteous pride.

"I didn't know I had it in me," she said.

"Oh, you do," I assured her. "In spades."

"Do I look scary, though?" said Rufus.

"You look big," I said. "And that's enough."

"Yeah, but I look big and sweet," said Rufus. "At least that's what my mom always told me. Like a big, cuddly sweetheart."

"These crooks don't know that you're a big cuddly sweetheart, though, do they?" I said. "They see a big dog and naturally assume you're a monster that's going to tear them limb from limb."

Rufus laughed a self-deprecating laugh. "Tear them limb from limb! I faint at the sight of blood, Max. I can't even catch a fly!" And he laughed a booming laugh at so much preposterousness.

And that's how we went into battle: one big blorange floofball, a smallish Ragamuffin, a tiny Yorkie and a gentle giant. Yikes!

CHAPTER 7

Aurelie hadn't asked to come on this honeymoon. She hadn't asked to travel all the way from Berlin, Maryland by plane to this godforsaken place called Hampton Cove. But Regarda had brought her along regardless, because that's what Regarda did: whenever she got an idea, she had to carry it through, consequences be damned, even if it meant inconveniencing the apple of her eye, the light of her life, her sweet darling Aurelie.

And since there wasn't a lot Aurelie could do about the situation, she decided to go with the flow and accept the unacceptable. It wasn't going to last forever. Only seven days. Ed didn't have the money to spend a fortnight at this swanky place anyway. Seven days was all he could afford, so seven days it was. Now if only she wasn't locked up in this here hotel room she could have borne things with more equanimity. But as it was, all she had to work with was this tiny room with its tiny balcony where she could see some of the sights.

"Oh, well," she sighed dramatically as she lounged on said balcony and glanced down at the world below. People were passing by. Cats and dogs were roaming wild and free. And only she was stuck up here with Ed and Regarda.

Up above on the roof, pigeons were squawking, probably making fun of her as she sat there, lonely and forlorn while Ed and his mom were out and about, painting the town red. Why they would want to paint the town red and not some other color Aurelie did not know, but then Regarda possessed an eccentric streak.

And she had sat there for what felt like an interminable length of time when suddenly a knock sounded at the door. She glanced up, wondering if Regarda and Ed had finished with their paint job already. It was hard to imagine, since painting an entire town sounded like a longish proposition. Expensive, too.

Another knock, this one a little louder. And then the door gently squeaked open and a person Aurelie had never seen before walked in. It was a man and he was dressed in black jeans, a black turtleneck sweater and black gloves. Even his shoes were black. He didn't look like any of the cleaners Aurelie had seen come and go since they booked into this hotel. He didn't look like room service either.

The man quietly proceeded into the room, glancing left and right as if looking for something. Maybe he was a friend of Ed's? Ed had a lot of friends, and all of them had offered their support when his marriage with Sara had been canceled. Then when Ed had become a YouTube sensation they'd also been in touch, this time congratulating him on a job well done. They seemed to believe that Ed had posted that video on purpose to get back at Sara somehow. Sara herself hadn't been in touch, though. Apparently she'd had a change of heart. Or at least that's what Regarda said. Which was too bad for Ed. Sara's original heart had been wildly in love with him, but this second heart, the one they had replaced the original one with, clearly not so much.

Aurelie had suggested Sara should demand her old heart back, or at the very least get a refund, for the new heart was clearly a bust, but of course no one ever listened to her.

The man had reached the balcony and now came face to face with Aurelie. A slow smile spread across his features, and Aurelie greeted him by inclining her head. After all, any friend of Ed was a friend of hers. But then this friend did the most outrageous thing: out of nowhere he suddenly produced a shopping bag, grabbed Aurelie, and without preamble or invitation stuffed her into the bag and zipped it shut!

And just when she thought her life couldn't get any worse.

* * *

Contrary to my instructions, Dooley was the first to go in. I had told him I should go first, since I was the one who knew where Johnny and Jerry might be holed up, but Dooley was raring to go and catch these miscreants in the act.

"I'll catch them for you, Max, just you wait and see!" were his last words before he disappeared from sight, his exit covered by the waist-high brambles and weeds—a human waist, that is, not my waist.

"I thought we were supposed to find them and scare them," Fifi said.

"That was the plan," I said.

"Clearly Dooley has another plan in mind," said Rufus, a touch of admiration in his voice for our intrepid friend.

"I hope he doesn't get lost," said Fifi, who didn't seem to

have a lot of faith in Dooley's skills as a leader in this crime-busting campaign.

"He won't get lost," said Rufus. "Dooley is a cat and cats never get lost. Isn't that right, Max? In that sense you guys are just like us dogs, right?"

My hesitation revealed my reluctance to endorse this theory, and Fifi laughed. "Cats can get lost, Rufus, just like humans. It's only dogs that can always be relied upon to find their way home."

"I'm sure cats can find their way home, too," said Rufus.

"Oh, they can find their way home, all right," said Fifi. "Providing you don't drop them off too far away. Put a cat on the other side of town and they won't be able to find their home if you put a big sign in front of them indicating the direction." She gave me a gentle smile. "Isn't that right, Max?"

"I'm sure that might be true for some cats," I agreed, "but most of us have an excellent sense of direction. In fact our sense of direction is probably superior to that of your own species."

"As if," Fifi scoffed.

"Can you two be quiet for a moment?" said Rufus suddenly. "I thought I heard something."

And so Fifi and I both piped down. We could always resume our 'Cats versus Dogs' discussion at a later date. And that's when I heard it: faintly but distinctly, soft cries could be heard. It wasn't clear to me whether the one producing them was a person or a pet, but it was definitely coming from somewhere nearby.

"It sounds like someone is in trouble," said Fifi.

And even though our mission was to try and capture Jerry and Johnny in the act, a unanimous decision was made to trace the source of this upsetting sound.

We might not be St. Bernards, and we might not be

carrying a barrel of brandy around our necks, but we are still eager to assist. And so we moved in single file toward the source of the sounds of distress and soon reached it. Picture our surprise when we found ourselves face to face with... an infant!

"It's a baby," said Fifi, who couldn't believe her eyes.

"A human baby," said Rufus, who's a stickler for accuracy.

"What is it doing here?" I asked, glancing around in a bid to locate the infant's parent pair.

"Maybe it got lost?" Rufus suggested. "Babies do get lost. Especially on the beach. They crawl off when their parents aren't looking and before you know it they've got everyone combing the beach and organizing a search party."

"This isn't the beach, though," said Fifi, and we couldn't argue with that. "Whoever lost this baby must be someone who lives on this block."

"I've never seen this baby before," I said.

"Me neither," said Rufus.

"Same here," said Fifi. "Which doesn't mean anything. There's new babies being born every day. Impossible to keep track of them all."

"Plus, all babies look the same," said Rufus. "Well, they do," he added when Fifi gave him an odd look. "Human babies, at least."

"What other kind is there?" said Fifi.

"Well, dogs have babies."

"They're called puppies, not babies."

It's true though that all babies do look the same, but I still pride myself in being able to make the distinction from one baby to the next. My own humans Odelia and Chase had decided to get into the baby business themselves recently, so I guess I'm something of a specialist in the curious phenomenon. Hence my comment that I'd never seen this baby before. Of that I was fairly certain.

"Maybe this baby just moved here?" Rufus suggested.

"Babies don't move anywhere on their own," Fifi said. "Everyone knows that babies are helpless creatures, and without their mommies and daddies they're completely lost. Now puppies, on the other hand—"

But before she could finish her sentence, the baby had opened its throat and was wailing away, clearly not happy to be sitting there in the middle of some field surrounded by two dogs and a cat.

Suddenly Dooley burst upon us, emerging from the high weeds and looking a little distressed. "Oh, there you are!" he cried. "I got lost, you guys. Where did you suddenly go—ooh! A baby!"

"Yes, a baby, Dooley," said Fifi with a smile. "How about that?"

Dooley looked from me to Fifi to Rufus. "Did any of you guys…"

We all laughed heartily. "Dooley, cats and dogs don't produce babies," I said. "Babies are strictly a human prerogative. Plus, it takes time to make a baby."

"I thought you would have seen that on your Discovery Channel," said Fifi.

"It's not *my* Discovery Channel," said Dooley with a touch of defensiveness. "And besides, Gran never lets me watch stuff like that."

"Stuff like what?" asked Rufus.

"Well, babies and stuff. She says that's for grown-ups only."

It was true that every time a documentary that dealt with the mystery of procreation aired, Gran turned off the television. She figured Dooley was too young to watch such content, and I happen to agree with her on that assumption.

"Okay, so if none of you made this baby, then who did?" Dooley demanded now. "And where are they, these baby-makers?"

"They must be around somewhere," said Rufus.

"And they're probably frantic with worry right now," said Fifi.

"So slight alteration in our mission plan," I said. "Instead of trying to collar a pair of wannabe burglars, we're going to bring this baby home to its parents."

"Its? I thought babies were either male or female?" said Dooley. Then his eyes widened. "Or are they like the banana slug!"

"The banana slug?"

"Yes, the banana slug is a simultaneous hermaphrodite, meaning it's both male and female at the same time." He stared at the baby. "I'll bet this baby is a simultaneous hermaphrodite. It's got that look. The look of a banana slug."

It was true that the baby had finally piped down, and was listening intently to our most interesting conversation. Or maybe it had never seen cats or dogs before and was trying to figure out if we were edible or not. I wouldn't go so far as to say it looked like a slug, though, banana or otherwise.

"So what's the plan?" asked Fifi, on whom this conversation was having an adverse effect. I guess she never watches the Discovery Channel.

But before I could speak, a butterfly approached us and settled down on the branch of a nearby tree. I recognized her as Flora.

"Hey, Max," she said by way of greeting. "Who are your friends?"

"Fifi, Rufus and Dooley," I said obligingly. "Fellas, this is Flora and she's a butterfly."

"We can see that," said Fifi as she studied the butterfly with interest. "You wouldn't happen to know who left this baby out here, would you?" she asked. "I mean, you butterflies probably get around a lot, right?"

"If by 'getting around a lot' you mean we fly hither and thither with not a care in the world, then yes, we do," said Flora with a laugh. "Though to be honest I've never seen this baby before."

"Shoot," said Fifi. "So now what?"

"Now one of us stays with the baby, making sure it doesn't come to any harm," I said, "and the rest go in search of its parents. Conversely, one of us goes in search of the parents while the rest stay here."

"I could go and look for the parents if you want," Flora suggested. "I have the bird's eye view, after all, and should be able to cover more ground more quickly."

The offer was gratefully accepted, but as we watched Flora flutter off, Dooley said, "Let's hope she doesn't get eaten by that bird's eye view."

CHAPTER 8

Regarda was relaxing on the beach, lounging in her lounger and gazing out across the expanse of ocean, when her phone dinged and a message appeared that sent shivers down her spine in spite of the hot day.

'Have Aurelie. You can get her back in exchange for 50k. No cops!'

"Ed!" she cried immediately, and shoved her phone in her son's face. Ed, who had been moping on the lounger next to hers, took the phone and read the message and smiled. "It's spam, Mom. Just block the number." He handed back the phone. "How many times do I have to tell you? The world is full of spammers."

"So how did they know that my cat is named Aurelie? Huh?"

This gave her son pause, for his frown had returned. "Well..."

"Let's go," she said, and was out of her lounger and stuffing her towel into her beach bag within seconds. The thought of someone having taken her precious baby was simply too much to bear! She loved her son, but sometimes she thought she might love Aurelie even more. At least she never gave her any trouble, or got dumped at the altar by a treacherous, duplicitous fiancée.

Without waiting for Ed, she scrambled through the hot sand, and was already at the stairs leading up to the boardwalk while he was still struggling to put on his T-shirt and cargo shorts over his wet trunks.

"Come on!" she cried as she mounted the wooden stairs. "I want to know if that bastard took my precious Aurelie or not!"

And then she was hurrying along the boardwalk, and heading into town where their hotel was located. One good thing about Hampton Cove was that the downtown area wasn't all that far removed from the beach. You could get there in next to no time, which was one of the many assets the Star Hotel boasted. But by the time Regarda had reached the corner of Main Street and Downey Street, she was already huffing and puffing. Her legs were too short for such an endeavor, and her body too round. Lucky for her, Ed came to her support and lent her his arm. Together they hurried on, and before long had reached their destination.

The moment they set foot in their hotel Regarda headed for the desk. "Did you see anyone leave the hotel with a pet cage by any chance?" she asked, her voice shaky from both the exertion and anxiety. When the receptionist answered in the negative, she hurried to the elevator. Rising to the third floor seemed to take an eternity, but finally they got there and Ed, bless him, was already running down the corridor, key card in hand, and when she got there had opened the door and was already calling out for Aurelie.

It didn't take them long to realize that her precious

darling was gone: there was only the one bedroom, one bathroom and one balcony. Nowhere to hide!

"She's gone," she said, sinking down on the bed. "They took my baby, Ed! Just took her like that!"

"We'll get her back," Ed said. "Don't you worry, Mom. We'll get Aurelie back."

"Fifty thousand, Ed! I don't have that kind of money."

"No, me neither," Ed admitted.

But then Regarda got an idea. "That ring you bought—did she give it back?"

"You mean Sara's engagement ring? No, she didn't."

"That cost you a pretty penny, didn't it?"

"Oh, but I couldn't possibly..."

"She left you, Ed! She left you standing at the altar like a fool!"

"I know, but..."

"Get it back—call her right now and get that ring back!"

"Okay, fine, but shouldn't we go to the police first?"

"Didn't you read the message? No cops, Ed—no cops!"

She watched as Ed took out his phone, walked out onto the balcony, and closed the door behind him. He didn't look happy about contacting the woman who broke his heart, but then desperate times call for desperate measures. She had some savings, Ed had some savings, she could borrow some money from her banker, who was her cousin, and together with that ring they just might make it.

But now who in their right mind would do such a thing? Who!

* * *

ODELIA SAT behind her desk and watched the news items appear on the Gazette website, one after another. All of them personally signed off for publication by Dan but not written by her. In fact no item that had appeared today had been written by her. Instead a small army of social media folks had supplied the copy.

She haphazardly scrolled through the list. There was an item about a frog that was found swimming in someone's bathtub. An item about someone's arthritis that was cured by a new miracle cure from Cambodia. An item about a secret alcove that was discovered in St. John's Church. And on and on and on it went.

She should have been out there, collecting stories and hammering out her own articles—earning her keep. But instead she was in here feeling sorry for herself and checking job sites for job openings. Because if this kept up the ax would fall on her employment, that much was obvious. She was sure Dan hadn't launched this new venture as a way to diversify but to save money. And that in his desire to economize he wouldn't hesitate to cut his biggest expenditure: her paycheck!

Her phone buzzed and she picked it up. "Hey, babe."

"Any news?" asked her husband.

"Nothing official," she said. "But I have a feeling I'll be out of a job by the end of the week."

"Bummer. At least you'll get severance pay, right?"

"I wouldn't bet on it. Knowing Dan he'll find a way to wriggle out of it. I passed his office this morning and heard him on the phone with what sounded like an employment lawyer. He's taking legal advice, Chase, and since he only has one employee, I'd say he's trying to get rid of me one way or another, and as soon as possible."

"He can't do this to you, babe. You practically write that entire paper."

"Not anymore. His experiment, as crazy as it sounds, seems to be working. He's getting copy from all over the place about all kinds of stuff that's going on in town and he doesn't have to pay these people a dime. They're happy to see their name in print. Delighted. In fact it wouldn't surprise me if Dan won't start charging *them* money."

"That can't be right."

"I know, but it's happening."

"Oh, dear, as your mother would say."

"You can say that again. What are we going to do?"

"We'll figure it out. You're not out of a job yet, are you?"

"Like I said, he's taking legal advice, so that doesn't bode well."

"We'll figure it out," Chase repeated, and because he sounded so sure of himself, she allowed herself to be reassured. But the moment she put down her phone and refreshed the Gazette website and saw a bunch of fresh news items spring up like daisies in a meadow, she was back to biting her nails.

CHAPTER 9

We'd been sitting watching the baby for a little while now and of Flora there was no trace.

"I think she forgot about us," Fifi declared.

"Yeah, she probably saw a nice flower and got busy collecting nectar," said Rufus. "Isn't that what butterflies do? Collect nectar?"

"I'm sure they do lots of things," I said vaguely, for I didn't have the slightest inkling what it was that butterflies actually occupy their time with. Apart from organizing races, of course.

"Butterflies eat bugs," said Dooley. "At least that's what I think they do. They eat bad bugs and make the world safe for democracy."

I had no idea what democracy had to do with butterflies but I wasn't in the mood to argue so I let my friend's comment slide.

The baby had settled down somewhat, and was still studying us intently. It seemed to have developed a keen fascination for our tails, and kept trying to grab mine. I knew from experience that babies have a strong grip, so I made sure that the little tyke didn't grab hold of this most sensitive appendage by flicking it to and fro but especially fro, if you catch my drift.

"What's taking her so long!" Fifi said. "I have better things to do than to spend my time babysitting, you know."

"Same here," said Rufus, who had assumed a restful position on the ground and was lazily swatting away the odd fly from time to time. "Plenty of stuff to do. People to see, places to go." He yawned. "Busy, busy, busy."

Somewhere nearby a cricket chirped and by all rights I should have found the sound soothing and sleep-inducing, but as these past couple of days had proved, sleep was still an elusive proposition.

"I've had it," said Fifi finally, and jumped up from her position next to the infant. "I'm sure this baby doesn't need the four of us to keep it out of harm's way. You guys can manage? Good. See ya."

And with these words she took her leave, causing more than a few looks of consternation amongst the remainers.

"I don't see what's so urgent that Fifi couldn't stick around for another couple of minutes," said Rufus, who must have felt a keen sense of abandonment now that his canine friend had left. "I mean, she's not as busy as all that, is she?"

"Maybe she has an important meeting planned," Dooley suggested. "Odelia always has important meetings planned, and she gets all worked up when she's running late for those meetings. Isn't that so, Max?"

"That is indeed so," I confirmed.

"Da da!" the baby said by way of endorsement of this view.

"See? Even the baby says I'm right," said Dooley.

"I'm pretty sure Fifi doesn't have any meetings planned," said Rufus. "Except maybe a meeting with her food bowl."

More time passed, and apart from the crickets, not a creature stirred.

"I think it's kind of relaxing," said Dooley. "The three of us spending some time in this field with this baby, I mean. Have you figured out the Terrific Word yet, Max? Now that you've had some time to think?"

"No, I have not," I admitted. Between the crooks I wanted to catch and this baby we needed to watch, all thought of soporific words had slipped my mind.

"I'll bet it's something very simple," said Dooley.

"What's all this about a word?" asked Rufus.

"Well, the four of us have been unable to go to sleep," I explained. "And this morning I suddenly remembered that someone once told me that there exists a so-called Master Soporific Word that when you utter it you immediately go to sleep. So now I've been trying to remember the word, because frankly we're all pretty exhausted at this point and I wouldn't mind taking a nice long nap."

"A Master Soporific Word," Rufus repeated thoughtfully. "I have to say I've never heard of such a thing, Max. Are you sure it's not one of those urban myths? You know, like the Yeti and the Abominable Snowman?"

"Who's the Yeti and who's the Abominable Snowman?" asked Dooley without missing a beat.

"I think the Yeti and the Abominable Snowman are one and the same," I ventured. "Two names for the same creature."

"It's a myth," said Rufus. "The Yeti doesn't actually exist."

"But what is it?" Dooley insisted.

"Well, it's supposed to be this big hairy ape-like creature that roams the Himalayas," said Rufus. "Or at least that's what they said in this movie we watched the other night. Ted is something of a horror fan, you see, and so we get plenty of that around our place."

"Odelia and Chase love horror movies, too," I said. "I can't even count the number of movies where I had to close my eyes and hide behind the couch."

"And me!" said Dooley. "Remember the one about the monster from the deep, Max? It lived in the deep and it was a monster," he explained for Rufus's sake. "But sometimes it got hungry and then it left the deep to go hunt submarines and such. It was very big and scary. I guess it liked the taste of cold hard steel."

"I wouldn't know," I said. "I was hiding behind the couch from the moment the monster first appeared on screen."

"It's the music, mainly," said Dooley, the horror movie aficionado. "Chase says that if you turn off the sound the movie isn't scary at all."

"Da!" said the baby, confirming this view on the filmmaking process.

Talking about monsters from the deep and scary sounds, suddenly a particularly scary sound emanated from deep inside the surrounding weeds. When it reached our ears, we all jumped about a foot in the air.

"What was that!" Dooley cried, immediately moving closer to me. "It's a monster, Max! It's the Bumbling Snowman!"

"The *Abominable* Snowman lives in the Himalayas, Dooley," I said. "If he exists at all, that is."

But it was true that something terrible seemed to be present nearby, and when a second eruption of sound rose up, it made my teeth chatter! And I didn't have a couch to hide behind!

"It's coming closer!" said Rufus, who had risen from his position and was standing at attention, looking this way and that and generally assuming a watchful stance.

"It's the Yeti," said Dooley in quivery tones, and I could tell that he was trembling with fear of what was to come.

"Dada!" the baby exclaimed, and seemed more excited than scared at the prospect of whatever monster was lurking in these weeds to come upon us and devour us whole!

"Shhh!" I admonished the little tyke. "Now is not the time to start talking, little one. Now is the time to be quiet as a mouse. And a quiet mouse, at that!"

But the baby wasn't deterred. Instead, it doubled down and started yelling, "Dada! Dada! Dada!" like some kind of broken record.

Another loud scream rose up, and this time it sounded too close for comfort.

"It's here!" said Rufus, as if we couldn't determine that for ourselves. "Save yourselves! Women and children first!" And then he did the most amazing thing: he carefully bit down on the baby's collar, picked it up and carried it off into the bushes!

"Did you see that, Max?" asked Dooley, fascinated in spite of our predicament. "Rufus is a St. Bernard!"

"He is," I agreed. "All that's missing is the little barrel of brandy."

But then another loud scream warned us of impending doom, and so we quickly followed in Rufus's wake, and skedaddled as fast as our legs could carry us. Yeti or no Yeti, I didn't want to find out what this thing could be!

Unfortunately for us, the baby hadn't received the

memo about things to do when you're being chased by a monster, for it kept up its mantra of 'Dada dada dada!'

As a consequence, the monster had a pretty good idea of where we were going, and kept up the pursuit. And judging from the thrashing sounds behind us, it was making good time and gaining on us!

CHAPTER 10

Harriet was finally on the verge of falling asleep when a loud scream rent the air and she was instantly wide awake again.

"Did you hear that?!" she said.

"Did I?" Brutus grumbled. "Almost as if someone is being strangled."

"Max and Dooley are out there," said Harriet. She exchanged a look of concern with her mate. "You don't think..."

"Let's go," said Brutus curtly.

They might not always see eye to eye with Max, and a good deal of ribbing and gentle remonstrations might be exchanged between the housemates, but that didn't mean they'd let any harm come to him.

And so the two of them hurried in the direction the terrible sounds seemed to be coming from: the field that stretched out behind the fence at the end of the garden. To hop onto the fence and over was but the work of a moment for both cats, for even when tired, they still possessed the necessary wherewithal to come to the aid of a friend.

"It's coming from that direction," said Harriet, and led the way. She didn't care that her perfectly groomed white fur became an attraction point for burrs and seeds. Abhorrent as the experience might be, she would deal with that later, once they had ascertained that Max and Dooley were safe, and not the victim of some terrible monster preying on innocent pets.

They streaked through brush and weed and soon were on the trail. And when finally they were upon the source of the blood-curdling and bone-chilling sound, they were much surprised to find that it belonged to… a human. And not a horribly deformed or monstrous human either, but Maggie Pearce, a recent arrival on Harrington Street.

"Jackie!" the woman was screaming, and she did indeed look and sound a little berserk, Harriet thought. "Jackie, where are you!" she screeched.

"It's not a monster," said Brutus, much sobered now that they had witnessed the source of those terrible screams with their own eyes.

"Who's Jackie?" asked Harriet. "And where are Max and Dooley?"

"Jackie!!!" Mrs. Pearce screamed.

"Max!" Harriet cried.

"Jackie!" Maggie Pearce yelled.

"Max!" Harriet repeated.

Mrs. Pearce had caught sight of Harriet and Brutus, and eyed them with a touch of concern. "You wouldn't happen to have seen my little girl, would you? She crawled out of our backyard just now. She's just a baby, for crying out loud!"

And crying out loud, she most certainly did, Harriet

thought. She shook her head. "Nope, we haven't seen any babies, have we, sweetie?"

"No babies," Brutus confirmed. "Max did see two crooks, didn't he, sugar plum? Getting ready to burgle our homes? Maybe they took this baby?"

"I doubt it," said Harriet. "Why would two burglars steal a baby?"

"For money?" Brutus suggested. "Babies get stolen all the time. It's called kidnapping, sweet pea."

"I know what kidnapping is, honey bunch," said Harriet with a touch of pique. "But Johnny and Jerry aren't kidnappers, are they?"

Brutus shrugged. "They might be branching out. Times are tough for crooks. Maybe the burgling field is getting crowded and they need to diversify. You know, expand their reach."

It was possible, of course, though unlikely, that Johnny and Jerry would have stooped so low as to enter the potentially lucrative field of kidnapping. Still, humans never cease to amaze and surprise, so it was certainly something to take into consideration.

A man had now joined them, and Harriet recognized him as Mark Pearce, Maggie's husband and presumably the father of the missing baby.

"Anything?" he said, panting a little as if from engaging in some track and field athletics. He was dressed in a tracksuit, so that seemed to fit the state he was in: sweaty brow, and a sort of wild look in his eyes.

"Nothing," said Maggie, a note of desperation in her voice.

"I thought I heard her call out to me before," Mr. Pearce said, placing his hands on his knees and catching his breath. "I ran in the direction of the sound, but it kept moving away from me, and I lost track."

Maggie Pearce wrung her hands and screwed up her face in an expression of extreme dismay. "You don't think she was... taken?"

Her husband shook his head. "I don't know what to think right now. But I do think it's time we called the police, don't you?"

Maggie seemed to hesitate. "It'll be all over the papers. It'll be such a big fuss. And the whole neighborhood will get involved. They'll think we're bad parents for allowing Jackie to get away."

"We're not bad parents," said Mark emphatically. "We took our eye off her for one second, and she's been a lively one from the day she was born." He smiled a half-smile. "I can't believe she snuck off on us like that."

"Snuck off on me, you mean," said Maggie, distraught to the extreme. "I let her get away, Mark. I'm a bad mother."

"Don't say that, honey. It could have happened to anyone. Now let's call the police and get some help. This is a pretty big field and she could be anywhere by now." His expression clouded. "If she wasn't kidnapped, that is."

"Oh, God," said Maggie, and buried her face in her hands.

"We have to help them, snuggle pooh," said Harriet.

"Us?" said Brutus, much surprised. "But we're not dogs, snuggle bug. Finding stuff is what dogs do, not cats. And besides, we don't have the energy."

Harriet pinned her mate with a steely look. "We're going to find that baby, Brutus, if it's the last thing we do. We have a responsibility to the residents of this neighborhood, whether we like it or not. So are you with me or not?"

"If you put it that way..." Brutus murmured, and meekly padded along in her wake.

"Now where would a baby go?" she asked.

"Where does anybody go?" asked Brutus with a touch of belligerence. He clearly wasn't in the mood to organize a search party.

"Ooh, I've got it!" said Harriet. "Why don't we ask Grace? She's still a baby herself, isn't she? And who better to get into a mind of a baby than a baby?"

"I like your thinking," said Brutus. "But there's one problem with that. Grace is at the day care center. She won't be home for another couple of hours."

"And that's where you're wrong," said Harriet triumphantly. "Grace is staying with her Auntie Scarlett today. So all we have to do is go and get her and then we can get this search effort underway!"

CHAPTER 11

We'd been going for a while, trying to get away from that horrible sound of some giant crashing through the brush when Rufus indicated that he was tired and wanted to take a break. I could sympathize, of course. If I were to carry a human infant I'd get tired, too. Babies might not look like much, but they're heavier than you think. They're top-heavy, you see, with most of their weight located in the head. Not like a kitten, which is already nicely proportioned.

"Why are baby heads so big, Max?" asked Dooley, who had noticed the same phenomenon now that Rufus had carefully placed the baby on a bed of leaves and settled down to take a breather.

"I have no idea, Dooley," I said.

"I once read it takes their bodies a long time to catch up with their heads."

"It's not that big," said Rufus, as he studied the baby, who was now lying on its back and clawing at the air with a look of wonder on its face. "I've seen bigger heads on babies than this one."

"I think it's pretty big, as baby heads go," said Dooley as he approached the baby, carefully and slowly as if approaching a live grenade that might go off at any moment. "In fact its head is almost as big as the rest of it."

"Now you're exaggerating," I said with a yawn. I'd also stretched out on the ground and was wondering if this wouldn't be a good time to test another theory I'd had: that if you really can't sleep you should tire yourself out physically. That way the body takes control and decides it needs its rest and shuts down that annoying chattery brain.

I closed my eyes, but of course sleep still wouldn't come. Gah.

"Okay, so now that we saved this big-headed baby from the Yeti, what are we going to do with it?" asked Dooley, who clearly had no intention of going to sleep, and didn't even seem tired anymore.

"We're not going to do anything with it," said Rufus. "We're going to get it back to its parents and that's it."

"If only we knew who the parents are," I said.

"They'll come for it," said Rufus confidently. "Parents of babies always come to get them. Just like a cat will look for its kittens and a dog for its puppies. It's the parental instinct, if you will."

"The maternal instinct," I specified. "I doubt if you'll find a lot of male cats looking for their offspring. On the contrary. They don't seem all that bothered. And the same goes for dogs, Rufus, and don't you deny it."

"No, it's true," Rufus conceded. "The male of the species doesn't seem to possess a parental bone in his body."

"Have you ever considered to, you know, produce offspring?" I asked, having wondered about this possibility for a while now.

"Oh, no," said the big sheepdog with a shy little smile. "I don't think that's in the cards for me, fellas."

"Why not?" asked Dooley. "You and Fifi would make a pretty pair."

"Ha!" said Rufus. "Dooley, you're so funny!"

Dooley glanced at me, then back at Rufus. "I'm funny?"

"Very funny!"

"I didn't know I was funny," Dooley admitted, but still seemed pleased with the compliment. "I don't know a lot of jokes, and the ones I do know aren't very funny. Or at least I didn't think they were." He cleared his throat. "So an American, a Frenchman and a Belgian are on a plane—"

"I mean, Fifi is a dear, dear friend," Rufus said. "A dear, dear, dear, *dear* friend. And obviously we all love our friends, especially the ones who are very dear to us…" His voice trailed off and he frowned as if he had lost the thread of his argument. "Um…"

Dooley, who had waited patiently for Rufus to finish talking, resumed his joke. "So an American, a Frenchman and a Belgian are traveling on a plane. Says the American—"

"Do we spend an awful lot of time together?" Rufus said, piping up again. "Yes, we do. But that's only to be expected when you live so close to each other. And when your humans are neighbors. We see each other at the dog park, and on the street, and we pay each other visits all the time…" He petered out again.

Dooley waited a beat, then took a deep breath. "So an American, a Frenchman—"

"Okay, so I like her," said Rufus, erupting into speech again. "I'm going to come right out and admit it. I like Fifi. In fact I like her a lot." He gave us a sort of defiant look. "And so what? Huh? So what if I like her? I'm not afraid to say it, okay?" He threw his head back and bellowed: "I LIKE FIFI!" He heaved a sigh of relief. "There. I said it. I've been wanting to say it for a long time but was afraid to. I don't even know why, but there you have it. Are you happy now, Max?"

"Absolutely," I said. "And congratulations, Rufus. Fifi is a fine, um, a fine..."

"Dog," Dooley supplied helpfully.

"Thank you, Dooley," I said. "Yes, Fifi is a fine dog, and you couldn't wish for a nicer mate than her, buddy. So yes, I'm happy for you."

"The thing is, Max," said Rufus, his face sagging somewhat, "that I haven't told her about my feelings, you know. I haven't even dropped a hint. Not even a tiny one. I know she likes me as a friend, but nothing more."

"So maybe it's time for you to finally come out and tell her how you feel?"

"But what if she doesn't feel the same way about me as I feel about her?" he said with an expression of agony written across his features. "Then what? I'll have ruined a fine friendship. And we'll still see each other every day and it's going to be awkward. It's going to be weird. You can't come back from that."

"Do you want me to put out some feelers?" I asked. "Cautiously ask her how she feels about you? Then I can tell you and you can take it from there. And if she doesn't feel the same way about you as you feel about her, no harm done. But if she does..." I wiggled my whiskers meaningfully.

The smile that lit up the big dog's face was something to behold. "Would you do that for me, Max? Would you?"

"Of course, buddy. Anything for a friend."

Dooley took a deep breath. "So an American, a Frenchman and a Belgian..."

But the story of the three men on the plane would have to wait, for at that very moment an elephant came crashing through the brush. Though when we looked a little closer it wasn't an elephant, exactly, but Johnny Carew. He stared at us for a moment, then a grin spread across his face. "Jer! I found them!"

Next Jerry Vale hove into view, and when his eyes landed on us, he also grinned from ear to ear. "The boss will be happy," he announced, and proceeded to grab me and Dooley by the scruff of the neck, and dump us into a big burlap sack! He tied the top of the bag and next thing we knew we were stuck.

"Catch him, you idiot!" we heard Jerry yell.

There was the sound of a struggle and some furious barking, and I prayed that they wouldn't be able to catch poor Rufus the way they caught us. But after a few moments we heard the sound of heavy breathing next to us, and the voice of Rufus spoke. "Did they catch you guys?"

"Yes, they did," I said. "You?"

"Yeah, they caught me," he said, and there was a note of bitterness in his voice as he said it. "That big brute jumped right on top of me!"

"You should have bitten him," Dooley suggested.

"I wanted to, but they were too fast for me. Before I knew what was happening, they threw a bag over my head and that was it. Game over for Rufus."

"I wonder what they want with us," said Dooley.

It wasn't a big mystery what they wanted with us. "Money, Dooley," I said. "There's lots of money in catnapping."

"And dognapping," Rufus supplied sadly.

There was the sound of a baby crying, and all three of us said simultaneously, "And kidnapping!"

CHAPTER 12

Odelia had decided to drop by the police station to look for material for a new story. After all, the only way she could convince her boss not to make her redundant was to prove that she was a valuable asset. That the stories she delivered were a far sight better than the muck his army of social media fans could produce. Also, if people wanted to read what other Facebook users wrote they could go on Facebook. They didn't have to pay good money to Dan for the privilege of subscribing to the Gazette and read the same rehashed stories.

It actually surprised Odelia that Dan hadn't realized this flaw in his scheme yet. But then the editor was far too busy jubilating over his new cost-saving enterprise to notice this one glaringly obvious drawback.

She arrived at the police station at the same time as a young couple who seemed highly distraught—especially the woman. She recognized them as the Pearces: Maggie and Mark.

"Hi there," she said in passing.

"Odelia Kingsley, right?" said Mark, a serious look on

his face. "You're a reporter for the Gazette. Our baby is missing, Mrs. Kingsley. Somehow she got out of her crib and into the field that backs onto our garden and we can't find her anywhere. We've looked everywhere but nothing."

"Oh, but that's terrible," said Odelia. "You don't live that far from me, do you? Harrington Street..."

"Fifty-two," Mark supplied. "Just a couple of houses down from you guys. We met at the block party last month."

"Of course." She glanced at Dolores, who manned the reception desk, and was intently staring in their direction. "Have you told Dolores yet?" she asked. "What did she say?"

"No, we haven't filed a report yet," said Mark, who seemed to be doing all the talking, his wife visibly too upset to engage in conversation. "The thing is," he added, lowering his voice, "that Maggie is afraid people will think we're bad parents for allowing our little girl to wander off."

"Mark, don't say that!" Maggie immediately admonished her husband.

"Nobody is going to think that," said Odelia. "I mean, it could happen to anyone. It could happen to me." She thought on her feet. "Look, we'll get the neighborhood to organize a search party. How about that? How old is she?"

"Nine months," said Maggie in tremulous tones.

"She can't have gotten far then," said Odelia as she placed a comforting arm around the woman's shoulder. "We'll find her, Maggie."

"We have looked," said Mark. "We've looked everywhere, and at some point I thought I heard her calling out to me. I thought I heard 'Dada' a couple of times. But when I arrived she wasn't there. So now I'm thinking..." He swallowed nervously. "We're thinking..."

"She might have been taken," Maggie supplied. "Kidnapped."

"Oh, no," said Odelia, shaking her head. "I'm sure that's not the case. We're a pretty safe community around here, especially Harrington Street and the surrounding neighborhood." Though as she spoke the words, some incidents came to mind that immediately belied her own statement. But she didn't think it was prudent to bring to mind some of her own investigations from the recent past. It would only serve to upset the couple even more.

"So do you think we should file a report?" asked Mark.

"Absolutely. You go ahead and talk to Dolores over there. And in the meantime I'll call around and get people organized. How does that sound?"

"That sounds great," Maggie admitted, and gave her a watery smile. "I just want Jackie back, Odelia. I want her back now."

"And you will get her back," said Odelia. "Just you wait and see."

As she walked out, she practically stumbled over Kingman, who was on his way in.

"Odelia!" said the big cat. "Just the person I came to see!"

She looked around, making sure no one was watching, then lowered her voice and said, "I can't talk now, Kingman. I have a baby to find."

"Oh, you lost your baby, huh? Well, that's too bad," said Kingman sympathetically. "But don't you worry about a thing, honey. There's plenty of babies in the world. You just go and pick out another one. Lots of choice."

She gave him a stern look. Just like his human Wilbur Vickery, Kingman clearly wasn't Mr. Sensitivity. "See you, Kingman," she said, and made to leave.

"No, wait!" said the large cat as he waddled after her.

"I've got something important to tell you. A cat's been kidnapped. Or catnapped, or whatever you wanna call it."

She turned and glanced down at Max's friend. "Catnapped?"

"Sure. I happened to overhear—"

"Not here," she said quickly. "People will wonder why I'm talking to a cat. Meet me in the park in ten minutes. First bench to the right of the entrance."

"Will do," said Kingman, well pleased. He started to walk away, then turned. "Oh, about your baby—have you tried catnip? It works wonders to draw out cats, you know, so it might work on babies, too."

"Ten minutes, Kingman," she snapped, and turned on her heel.

It took her ten minutes to talk to Chase on the phone, and tell him to start organizing a search of the field behind the house, and to walk to the park to meet Kingman. When she arrived there, the big cat was already seated on the park bench, right in the middle, as if he owned the place.

"Oh, there you are," he said. "I thought you'd be a no-show."

"When I tell a person I'll meet them, I keep my promise, Kingman," she said as she took a seat next to the feline. "So what's all this about a catnapping?"

The cat became animated. "Yeah, so I was minding my own business out in front of the store, like I always do, when this lady walked past, accompanied by some young feller. The lady seemed very distressed, and she kept telling the guy that he should keep his mouth shut and stop going on about talking to the police. So naturally I pricked up my ears and paid close attention to what they were saying. And as luck would have it, they walked into the store and carried on their conversation with me right on their tail."

"Did you recognize them? Were they locals?"

"Tourists, I think. Mother and son. She asked him about a ring she wanted him to sell. An engagement ring, I believe. And he said some woman named Sara kept blocking his calls and texts. And then she came right out and said: 'If we don't get the money, they're going to feed Aurelie to the dogs, Ed. To the dogs! My sweet, precious baby!' And that's when it dawned on me that this Aurelie just might be a pet. Cause who'd want to feed a baby to the dogs, right?"

Odelia shivered when she contemplated the answer to that question. There probably were people around who were capable of such a horrible thing.

"And also, this woman looked old enough to be your mother, and I might not know a lot about human females, but I do know that at some point you guys stop popping out babies, right? What's the cut-off point these days? Forty? Forty-five? Well, this lady was probably late fifties, early sixties."

Odelia gave Kingman a stern look. "Please don't talk about people like that, Kingman. Show some respect."

"What did I say?" said Kingman innocently, spreading his paws.

"Okay, so you happened to overhear a man and a woman, possibly mother and son, discuss a possible kidnapping of a pet—dog or cat or in fact any other species. So what do you want me to do about it?"

"I don't know. You're the reporter. And as Max never stops reminding me, you're always on the lookout for a story. Well, here is a story for your paper. And you don't have to thank me," he added when she opened her mouth to respond. "Just tell Wilbur that I have a tummy ache, and that he needs to take me to see the vet." He slumped a little. "I mean, I've tried to tell him, but you know what most humans are like: they don't listen to a word you say."

Odelia softened. "I'll tell him to go and take you to see Vena," she said.

"Not that I *want* to see Vena, but this tummy ache can't be good."

"No, you should have that looked at," she stressed. "How long have you had pain in your stomach?"

"Um, couple of weeks maybe? It kinda comes and goes, but lately it comes more than it goes, if you know what I mean."

"I'll tell Wilbur to take you to see her right away," she said as she patted the cat on the head. "And thanks for telling me about this kidnapping. You did good, Kingman."

"Sure thing," he said. "They're staying at the Star Hotel, by the way. Just in case you want to go and pay them a visit. Third floor. I saw them on the balcony. And if I'm not mistaken I think I saw a cat up there. But I could be wrong. My eyes aren't what they used to be."

"You definitely have to see Vena."

Kingman sighed deeply. "Oy vey."

CHAPTER 13

Harriet and Brutus had finally arrived at Scarlett's apartment, and as luck would have it, Gran's friend's window was open and so when both Harriet and Brutus started mewling at the top of their lungs, the russet curly head of Scarlett appeared, and when she glanced down and saw that it wasn't some Romeo who stood serenading her but two cats, she smiled and said, "Wanna come up?"

"No, we don't want to come up," said Harriet. "We want Grace to come down and help us find a baby."

"Just one second," said Scarlett. "I'll buzz you in."

"Too bad there aren't more people who can speak our language," said Brutus as they stepped up to the front door of the apartment building and pushed themselves in. Soon a buzzing sound could be heard, and the inner door clicked open. Try as she might, though, Harriet couldn't wedge her way through. "Let me handle this," said Brutus, and gave the door a good shove. It soon saw the error of its ways and gave up the fight.

"Up here!" a voice caroled from upstairs. "Second floor!"

"And all this on an absolute lack of sleep," Brutus sighed.

"Maybe when this is all over," said Harriet as they started skipping up the stairs, "we'll finally be able to sleep."

"Let's hope you're right," said Brutus.

They reached the landing, and Scarlett greeted them at the door. "Now to what do I owe the pleasure of this visit?" she said as she escorted them into her humble abode. "Nothing happened to Vesta, I hope?" There was a touch of concern in her voice as she said this, but even if Harriet would have tried to put her at ease, she wouldn't have understood. So instead the white Persian went in search of Grace.

"Grace!" she said. "Grace, we need your help!"

"In here," a voice called out. "She put me in front of the TV!"

And true enough they found Grace in the living room watching television. It was some kids' show about cats in outer space that seemed interesting enough. But since time was of the essence, Harriet decided not to join the toddler on the couch.

"Is it any good?" asked Brutus, who didn't have such qualms. He had jumped up on the couch and settled in for the duration.

"It's not bad," said Grace. "But honestly, cats in space? Not very realistic!"

"Not really," Brutus admitted. "Though I could be enticed to join some NASA program to fly to the moon. Floating through space must be way fun. And I wouldn't mind sampling some of that space food. I'll bet it's yummy."

"Can we please focus here?" said Harriet. "Grace, a baby has gone missing, and we need your help to find it."

The little girl stared at her. "You need my help finding a missing baby?"

"Uh-huh, that's right."

"I mean, I don't mind giving you a helping hand," said Grace with a frown. "But I'm not exactly an expert on finding people. Are you sure you shouldn't be talking to the police? In other words: my dad?"

"We would, but he's at work, and so is your mom, and the rest of the family. You're the closest person we could think of who can speak our language."

"Plus, you're a baby yourself so you're best placed to find other babies," Brutus pointed out as he took a lick from the dish Scarlett had placed in front of Grace and made a face. "Yuck. What is this stuff?"

"Beef and carrots. What do you mean: I'm a baby so I can find other babies?"

Brutus gave her a blank look. "Isn't it obvious? You're a baby. So you just go out there and sniff out this missing baby. Easy peasy."

Grace smiled a gummy smile. "It doesn't work like that, Brutus."

"It doesn't?"

"No, it does not. You're confusing me with a dog. Unlike a dog I don't have a superior sense of smell that allows me to find other babies."

"I know you're not a dog," said Brutus. "But you're a baby."

"So?"

"Well, can't you, I don't know, sniff out other babies or something?"

Grace laughed, a pleasant sound, like ice cubes tinkling in a glass. "You think babies are all connected through some mysterious link? That there's a cell tower we hook up to? I'm not a cell phone, Brutus, or an alien who phones home!"

"No, I guess you're not," said Brutus as he eyed Harriet uncertainly as if to say: 'Now what?'

"Now we're stuck," said Harriet.

"Can I get you guys anything?" said Scarlett as she walked in from the kitchen. "I don't keep cat kibble, since I don't have a cat, but I do have some chicken in the fridge. I could put it in the microwave if you want."

It sounded pretty enticing, and under different circumstances Harriet would have said yes in a heartbeat. But she felt responsible for this missing baby. And if Grace wasn't going to help them find it, they needed to go and talk to Odelia. And since they'd already wasted a lot of time, they needed to get going ASAP.

"No, thank you," she said therefore. "A baby went missing, and we need to find her."

"I wouldn't mind a piece of chicken," said Brutus.

"Later," Harriet said. "When we have found the baby."

"I'll pop it into the microwave, shall I?" said Scarlett.

"No, that's fine," said Harriet, waving a paw. "Next time."

"Great. I'll do that right now," said Scarlett, well pleased.

"But we don't want chicken!" said Harriet. But of course Scarlett had already disappeared. Harriet turned to Grace. "Can't you tell her we need to go?"

"I wish," said Grace. "For some reason I can talk to you guys, but the human language? I'm still a long way from taming that particular beast!"

"God, why is this so complicated!" said Harriet, feeling frustrated.

"Oh, relax," said Brutus. "Take a load off and eat some

chicken. That baby isn't going anywhere, is it? And besides, by now its parents are probably talking to Uncle Alec, and he's setting up roadblocks all over town."

"People don't set up roadblocks for missing babies, snuggle bear. They organize search parties."

"Exactly!" said Brutus. "Search parties, dragnets—whatever. I'm sure they'll be able to find one tiny, teeny baby. After all, humans are well-equipped to deal with these little emergencies. Babies wander off all the time. Isn't that right, Grace?"

"We do have a tendency to wander off," Grace admitted. "To go and explore. See the world. Discover new and exciting sights and sounds..." She sighed. "The world *is* a fascinating place, isn't it?"

"Isn't it just?" Brutus agreed, and gave that dish of baby food another lick.

CHAPTER 14

Vesta Muffin wasn't exactly known for possessing a compassionate streak, especially when it came to her son-in-law Tex. But today she actually felt sorry for the guy. All morning he'd been moping and complaining and looking miserable. And all because someone had damaged one of his gnomes—or two of them, to be precise. He'd even shown pictures to Vesta detailing the damage. An ugly gnome named Norbert had a piece of chewing gum attached to its face. And another one named Jackson Brown now went through life without a nose. Not that gnomes needed a nose. They weren't human, after all, so what did they need noses for?

But sensing that this was a delicate topic, she refrained from pointing out the obvious: that there are worse things in life than some damage being inflicted on a stupid garden ornament. Good thing tact and diplomacy came natural to her, or she would have told Tex to grow a pair and stop crying like a little baby.

"You can still see where the gum got into his eyes," said

Tex as he pinch-zoomed on Norbert's visage. "I got most of it off, but there's some left that needs to be professionally removed."

"You need paint thinner, that's what you need," said Vesta. "Just soak that big sucker in a bucket of paint thinner for a couple nights and that gum will come right off. He'll look as good as new."

"But all of his paint will come off!" Tex cried, aghast at this suggestion. "He'll look like he came out of the factory."

"Exactly!" said Vesta. "Factory reset. That's what you want."

"That's not what I want!"

Vesta suppressed a strong urge to give her son-in-law a thwack across the noodle. It was an urge she frequently got when dealing with her daughter's husband. "Okay, so don't use paint thinner. All the same to me. Now Mrs. Baumgartner will come in at two, and then..." A sound like a broken coffee grinder reached her ears. It took her a while to realize it was Tex. "Now what?"

"I can't deal with Ida, Vesta. Not today. Not when I'm worried to death about Norbert."

"Who's Norber—oh, the troll."

"Gnome."

"Whatever."

"Can't you tell her I'm unavailable?" he asked with a hopeful look.

"You're the doctor, Tex. You tell her."

"She won't believe me," he said somberly. "And even if she does, she'll still insist she needs to see me."

They shared a look. Ida Baumgartner had become the bane of both their existences, with her never-ending array of imaginary illnesses and her insistence she was at death's door and had to see the doctor right this minute or else.

"Maybe you could kill her," Vesta suggested. "It's probably not appropriate for a doctor to kill a patient, but sometimes you have to think outside of the box. And putting Ida in a box just might be the best thing that ever happened to her. Put her out of her misery." Put everyone out of their misery, she thought, herself first.

"Okay, so this conversation never took place," said Tex.

"Fine," she said with a shrug. "So you have Ida at two, and then Frank Parker—next is—"

"I'm going to install cameras!" suddenly Tex burst out, in an attempt to stop her from droning on about which patients he still had to see. Anything to escape reality.

"Cameras?"

"Cameras!" he said triumphantly. "Plenty of cameras. Let them try and hurt Norbert then. I'll catch them in the act and denounce them!"

"The days of pillorying people are long gone, Tex," she gently reminded him. "We've moved on from medieval times, you know. And besides, I thought you already put up cameras?"

"What are you talking about? I just had the idea this morning."

"I could be mistaken, but I thought I saw a bunch of cameras attached to the back fence when I went to put the kitchen scraps in the compost bin."

Tex stared at her. "Cameras? On *my* back fence?"

"I wouldn't call it *your* back fence. More like *our* back fence."

"Impossible."

"But still true."

She was startled when he hit his hand with his fist. "The bastard!"

"Huh?"

"Ted. He must have put up those cameras. To know when the coast is clear."

She was starting to worry about the man now, and placed a hand on his brow. No fever. But that didn't mean he wasn't sick. "Maybe you should go and lie down for a minute," she suggested.

"Oh, didn't I tell you? Ted is the one who destroyed my gnomes!"

"Destroy is a big word, Tex. It's just a piece of gum..."

"I see what's going on now."

"Then you see more than me."

"Ted installed his own surveillance system, and every time the coast is clear, he steps into *my* backyard and takes a whack at *my* gnomes!"

"Now why would he go and do a thing like that, huh?" she said as she took a closer look at the man's pupils. They weren't dilated. And no spittle was flying from his mouth either. Not yet, at least.

"Because he wants to win first place in this year's Gnome of the Year contest, that's why! And get his picture on the cover of *Gnome & Gardens*!"

"Is that a fact?" said Vesta, slowly backing away from the man. Clearly the poison was spreading rapidly. And so she decided to bring in the big guns. And while Tex raged on about his precious trolls—or gnomes—she picked up her phone from her desk. Moments later the call connected. "Marge?" she whispered into the device. "It has finally happened. Your husband has gone cuckoo!"

"I'm coming right over," Marge's response came back immediately.

"Gnomes, Marge," Vesta whispered. "It's all about the gnomes!"

"Oh, dear," said her daughter. "I knew this would happen one day. Can you handle him for another five minutes, Ma?"

"I'll try," said Vesta. "But when he turns violent, I'm bringing out my hockey stick."

"I'll be there in five. And whatever you do, don't mention Ted."

"Too late," she said as she watched Tex gesticulating wildly.

CHAPTER 15

"It's a little cramped in here."

"I know, Dooley," I said. "That's because we're in a bag."

"Why did Johnny and Jerry put us in a bag, Max?"

"I guess it's the customary thing to do when you're catnapping a pair of cats. It's probably chapter one in the catnapping manual."

"Oh." For a moment all was quiet, then he said, "So Johnny and Jerry are crooks again?"

"I guess that's a given."

"This redivism is tough."

"Recidivism. And yes, it does seem tough to beat."

We were in the back of a van, or at least I thought we were, judging from the noise of the engine and the fact that we kept being bounced around. At one point something bumped into me and Rufus's voice sounded very close when he said, "Apologies."

"Not your fault, Rufus," I said.

"I wonder if they put the baby in a bag, too," said Dooley.

"I doubt it," I said. "Babies are pretty harmless compared to cats or a big dog like Rufus. They don't need to be restrained the way we do."

"I would have come along willingly," said Dooley. "If they'd offered a nice meal I'd have accepted the offer. But they didn't ask. They just grabbed us and put us in this bag. Not very nice, Max. Not polite."

"Maybe they didn't recognize us. If they did, they would know we belong to Odelia, and they wouldn't be doing this."

"I don't belong to Odelia," said Rufus sadly. "So I guess they would have taken me regardless." Then an idea occurred to him. "Hey, maybe you guys can negotiate our release! I mean, you said you know these fellas, right?"

"We do, but unfortunately they won't be able to understand my offer," I said, feeling bad about raining on Rufus's parade. But it was probably best if we knew where we stood. "We'll either have to escape or we'll have to trust that Odelia will find us."

"Do you think she'll look for us, Max?" said Dooley. "She might be glad to be rid of us. We do cause her a lot of trouble sometimes, don't we?"

"Of course Odelia will come looking for us," I said. "She loves us, Dooley. And she'll want to bring us home as soon as possible."

"They'll probably demand a ransom," said Rufus. "That's what they do in cases like this."

"How much do they want for us?" asked Dooley.

"Oh, not a lot, I would guess," I said. "After all, our humans are not rich or famous or anything, so they know they can't afford to pay a big ransom for us."

"Ted and Marcie have some money saved up," said Rufus. "Though Ted keeps spending it on those gnomes of his, even though Marcie keeps telling him not to. Did you know that one gnome can cost upward of a thousand bucks? There's this one gnome that's very rare and costs 1500 dollars. That's one expensive gnome."

"Don't tell me Ted spends that kind of money on his gnomes?" I said.

"He doesn't. Marcie would kill him if he did. But he wants to. I catch him checking out these specialized websites. And of course he subscribes to *Gnome & Garden* and is a paying member of the Gnome Society. This year he hopes to win first prize in the Gnome of the Year contest. So he's been trying to get his hands on what he calls a winner. A gnome that will stand out and catch the jury's eye."

"There's a Gnome of the Year contest?" asked Dooley.

"Oh, sure. It's a traveling contest, in that it lands in a different part of the country every year. This year it's picked Hampton Cove, and of course tempers are already running high and gnome fever is in the air."

"Gnome fever," said Dooley with a giggle. "That's funny." Which reminded him. "Do you know the one about the American, the Frenchman and the Belgian who are traveling on a plane?"

"Maybe not now, Dooley," I said. "We're in serious trouble here, and if we don't figure out a plan of escape, we might be locked up for a very long time." I was more worried about the baby, though. We could take care of ourselves, but that poor infant needed its mommy and daddy. I'm not an expert on babies, but from what I could tell, this particular baby was still very young and vulnerable.

"Okay, so what's the plan?" asked Rufus. "How do we get out of this predicament?"

"I say our window of opportunity will be when they open these bags," I said. "So we should be ready to escape the moment they stop the van and let us out. I say we use any means necessary to escape. Scratching, clawing and biting—nothing is off limits as far as I'm concerned. So Rufus, practice your biggest bark and work those snappers until you're good and ready to pounce on these fellas."

"I thought they were your friends?" asked the big dog.

"I thought so, too. But obviously they're not," I said sadly.

"They used to work for Marge," Dooley explained. "Until they robbed the bank next door and escaped to Mexico with the money. Though we did meet them once when they joined the Jehovah's Witnesses, didn't we, Max?"

"There was still hope for them back then," I said with a sigh. A soft growling sound came from right next to me. "Is that you, Rufus?" I asked, wondering if there were other pets in there with us. Or babies. Though babies rarely growl.

"Yeah, I'm practicing, just like you said."

"Maybe we should practice, too," said Dooley. "It's been a long time since I scratched or bit someone, and I'm not sure I'll be able to do it."

"It's easy," Rufus assured him. "Just think they're a nice piece of steak and there's about a hundred other dogs—big, mean, hungry dogs—trying to get that same piece of steak, and if you don't dig your claws in deep, and your teeth, you'll lose your chance."

Dooley was quiet for a moment as he tried to picture the scene. "I see the steak," he said finally, "and I see the hundred big, mean, hungry dogs, but I have to be honest with you, Rufus. I don't see myself getting away with the steak in your scenario."

"Oh, Dooley," I said with a sigh.

CHAPTER 16

Marge and her mother regarded their patient closely. Tex seemed to have calmed down to some extent. When Marge arrived at the office he was still mumbling vague threats addressed to Ted, whom he seemed to consider Public Enemy Number One, but he wasn't foaming at the mouth, as Ma's phone call seemed to suggest, and neither was he violent or a danger to himself or others.

"He seems fine to me," she said therefore.

"He says Ted is destroying his gnomes," said Ma. "He says Ted installed a bunch of cameras so he can keep an eye on the backyard and when the coast is clear he comes and takes a big old whack at Bernard—"

"Norbert."

"—so he can win the Gnome of the Year contest."

Marge heaved a deep sigh. "I just wish that contest had never come to Hampton Cove. Ever since they made the announcement in *Gnome & Garden,* Tex hasn't been himself and neither has Ted. They seem to consider the other person their biggest competitor, when all the while it is in fact Blake Carrington they should watch out for."

"Carrington is into gnomes?"

"Big time. And if what I saw of his collection is anything to go by he's the one to beat. The surprise contender. But no. Tex and Ted have to keep slugging away at each other—figuratively speaking."

"You know what we should do? Organize an intervention. Maybe connect with Marcie and put both men on the spot."

It wasn't a bad idea, but frankly Marge didn't think it was necessary. Once this contest was over, and Blake Carrington had won the big prize, Tex and Ted would forget all about their animosity and maybe even throw in the towel for good.

"Or maybe I could take a hammer to those wretched gnomes," Ma suggested. "Put them out of their misery once and for all."

"You would suggest such a scheme, wouldn't you?" said Marge with a smile. It was exactly like her mother to suggest a radical solution to the problem.

"It'd break my heart, of course," said Ma virtuously. "But sometimes a mother-in-law has to do what a mother-in-law has to do to save her beloved son-in-law from doom." The corners of her mouth turned down. "Plus, I hate those trolls. They creep me out."

"They are a little creepy," Marge had to admit. "And can you imagine I have one of those trolls staring back at me every night when I go to sleep and every morning when I wake up?"

"You mean Tex?"

"No, I don't mean Tex, Ma. I mean that portrait of a gnome he insists on keeping in our bedroom."

"Do you want me to steal it? I have connections in the

underworld, you know. I could set something up for a price."

"*You* have connections in the underworld. Seriously, Ma?"

"I'm not kidding, honey. Remember Dick Bernstein? He used to work as a croupier in Las Vegas. And he keeps telling me the owner of the casino was this well-known crime boss who had his finger in a lot of pies. The kind of pies you don't want to know about. The stinky kind."

Marge made a face. "Ma."

"But it's true. If I ask Dick to stage a burglary and get rid of both that painting and those gnomes, consider it done. For the right price, of course."

"Of course." Ida Baumgartner had walked into the waiting room and both Marge and her mother greeted her from behind the desk.

"Ooh, quite the reception committee," Ida said. "What's the special occasion?"

"No special occasion," said Marge. "Just paying a visit to my mom and my husband."

Tex appeared at the door, drawn by the sound of voices, and plastered a weak smile onto his face. "Ida. So nice to see you," he said, but his voice lacked the true ring of conviction. "Come on in."

"Oh, Tex," said Ida as she followed the doctor into his inner office. "I've been suffering from piles. Big nasty ones. They have to be seen to be believed!"

The look of distress on Tex's face told Marge he was about to do exactly that, and he wasn't exactly looking forward to the prospect!

"Poor Tex," she said the moment the door was closed. "With a patient like Ida dropping by several times a week it's no wonder he's stressed."

Ma gave her a slight nudge. "If you want I could ask

Dick to get rid of Ida, too. I'm sure he wouldn't mind adding her to his hit list."

"God, Ma!" said Marge, rolling her eyes. "You're kidding, right?"

"Of course I'm kidding!" said Ma. "Do you honestly think I'd suggest that Dick starts killing off Tex's patients? I'm joking, hon!" Then a grim look crept up her face. "Besides, knowing Ida I'm pretty sure she'd prove impossible to kill. Women like that, suffering from a thousand ailments, tend to outlive us all."

Just then, Odelia came bursting into the office. She looked a little perturbed, Marge thought. Immediately she thought the worst. "Did something happen to Grace?"

"Grace is with Scarlett," Ma said. "She's fine."

"Have you seen the cats today?" asked Odelia.

"I saw them this morning—why?" said Marge.

"I just passed by the house and they weren't there. None of them. And I saw Kingman and he hasn't seen them either. So where are they?"

"They must be around somewhere," said Ma. "They never stray far from home. Have you looked upstairs? Lately they've started sleeping on the bed when we're not home. Nice and cozy."

"I've looked everywhere, Gran," said Odelia. "They're not home, they're not in town—they've all disappeared!"

"Have you checked the barbershop?" asked Marge.

"Buster hasn't seen them since last night."

"The police station?" asked Ma.

"Nope," said Odelia, shaking her head. "And they're not at the church either. I talked to Shanille and she hasn't seen them since cat choir." She raised her arms and dropped them to her sides. "They're gone! And with Jackie going missing I wanted to ask for their help finding her, but now it seems they've gone missing, too. And then there's Aurelie!"

Odelia's bottom lip was trembling and Marge placed an arm around her shoulder. "Hey," she said consolingly. "It's our cats. You know how resourceful they are. I'm sure they're fine."

"Who's Aurelie?" asked Ma. "And Jackie?"

"Jackie Pearce. Mark and Maggie Pearce's baby. She crawled out of her crib this afternoon and is missing. And Aurelie is a cat belonging to a couple of tourists staying at the Star Hotel. She's been taken and the kidnappers are demanding a ransom."

"A ransom!" Marge cried.

Odelia nodded. "I haven't spoken to Aurelie's owners, but Kingman told me the story. Apparently they're keeping quiet about it. Possibly the kidnappers told them not to contact the police. But I'm going over there now to talk to them. But first I thought I'd ask the cats to start looking for Jackie. She wandered into Blake Carrington's field and must have got lost."

"You go and talk to these tourists," said Marge. "Your grandmother and I will look for the cats and Jackie, all right?"

"Thanks, Mom," said Odelia with a watery smile. "I hope you find them. Those cats mean the world to me."

"They mean the world to us," Marge corrected her daughter. "And of course we'll find them. Because they're not lost—I'm sure of it."

CHAPTER 17

Aurelie didn't know where she was, but wherever it was, it wasn't very nice. The small space where she'd been confined had an odoriferous quality that didn't appeal to her sensitive sense of smell. It was a mixture that was entirely too rich for her taste, and reminded her of the times Regarda enjoyed a Chinese takeaway night, which happened all too frequently in Aurelie's personal opinion. There was also a hint of cigarette smoke and stale leftover pizza. All in all not the kind of environment to which she was accustomed.

The walls were held together by layers of peeling paint, there were exotic-looking spots on the ceiling that could only be described as moldy and the floor reminded her of one of Regarda's brothers' teeth. Uncle Earle hadn't visited a dentist in forty years and wasn't going to because he said all dentists are thieves.

She was relegated to a ratty blanket in the corner of the room, with nothing but a tin bowl filled with tap water and another tin bowl filled with cheap kibble—the store brand. For a cat used to drinking mineral water and the best kibble money could buy this unwanted sojourn was a pretty rude awakening.

Suddenly the bolt on the door was thrown and she assumed an attentive stance. Was this the moment she was finally saved from this ordeal? Was Regarda finally coming to her rescue? Or Ed?

But when the door opened, instead of being greeted by the sight of her human, instead she saw her kidnapper step into the room and quickly close the door behind him as he approached.

Aurelie shivered with apprehension. She didn't like this man. She didn't like anything about him. He smelled of cigarettes. And most importantly, he hadn't spoken a word since he made her acquaintance. In other words, not a gentleman!

This visit proved no exception. Instead of approaching her with kindness and a loving heart, he simply dumped more kibble into her bowl—once more from some cheap second-rate brand, she saw, and then did the oddest thing: he put a newspaper next to her, stepped back to take a picture with his phone, and removed the newspaper again. And as he made for the door, she said, her voice tremulous with emotion, "My litter box needs cleaning, sir. Could you please do the honors? I can't possibly go in a dirty litter box, now can I?" She gave him her best simpering smile, but to no avail. He didn't even give her a second glance, nor did he check her litter box. In fact he hadn't cleaned out her litter box since the moment she arrived in this terrible place.

And as he left the room and closed and bolted the door behind him, she took up her lonely vigil on that cold floor again. She was still hopeful her ordeal would come to an end soon—but not very.

* * *

Regarda was out of her mind with worry about her precious baby. Every moment Aurelie was out there was agony. She'd taken her in as a kitten, and the two hadn't been apart ever since. She adored the lovely creature, and now she was taken by some horrible person, and kept in circumstances that probably were too horrid to contemplate.

"And?" she asked as she halted her pacing for a moment to get a progress report from Ed.

"She keeps blocking me," said Ed sadly as he put down his phone. "I simply can't get through. I've tried her brother, her parents, her best friend, but clearly they've all been instructed not to talk to me or respond to any of my messages."

"Oh, for crying out loud," said Regarda, and grabbed her own phone. She still had Sara's mother's phone in her speed dial list, and called it now. She and Imelda had always gotten along great, and it would greatly surprise her if she would block her, too. But all she got was the woman's voicemail. "Look here, Imelda," she said, not brooking a lot of nonsense. "My sweet Aurelie has been kidnapped and the kidnapper wants fifty thousand for her safe release. So can you ask Sara to give Ed back that ring he gave her? If we sell it we might be able to raise that kind of money. If not…" She swallowed as she locked eyes with her son. "If not I will personally come down there and I will kick the living daylights out of that no-good daughter of yours. And I'm not even kidding. Not very much anyway."

"Mom!" Ed hissed as she disconnected.

"I don't know, Ed," said Regarda. "I'm at the end of my rope here. If we don't get that money—"

A knock at the door interrupted her.

Both she and her son looked up in alarm.

"The kidnapper!" said Regarda. "Maybe he had a change of heart. I knew this would happen. You can't look into Aurelie's eyes and not be moved by her grace and beauty and—who are you?"

Ed had opened the door and a woman stood on the threshold.

"My name is Odelia Kingsley," said the woman, who was fair-haired and slim and didn't look like a vicious catnapper at all. "I work for the *Hampton Cove Gazette* and—"

"A reporter!" Regarda cried.

"—I also assist the police in their inquiries from time to time as a civilian consultant. Someone overheard you and your son discuss the kidnapping of your cat, and so I wanted to offer you my services, since I'm a cat owner myself."

Regarda hesitated. "The kidnapper told us not to involve the police, but he didn't say anything about reporters, so..."

"The thing is," said this Odelia person as she stepped into the room, "that I have four cats myself, so I can understand how you feel, Mrs..."

"Cooper," said Regarda, accepting Odelia's outstretched hand. "Regarda Cooper. And this is Edgar, my son."

"We're worried sick," said Ed. "Aurelie was taken this morning, while we were at the beach, and the kidnapper sent a text demanding fifty thousand dollars."

"He sent you a text?" asked Odelia. "Can I see it?"

Regarda produced her phone and showed the text. "How did this person get your number? And how did he know you would be at the beach this morning and Aurelie would be all alone in the room?"

"You mean... you think it's someone we know?" asked Ed.

"Possibly. Or it could be someone from the hotel," said Odelia. "Someone who knows your schedule and has access to your personal data. Or maybe the kidnapper paid a member of staff to pass on that information." She thought for a moment. "Would you mind if I bring my husband in on this? He's a cop, but he's very discreet. He could talk to the hotel manager and make some inquiries."

"But the kidnapper said no cops," said Regarda. She shook her head. "I really don't want anything to happen to Aurelie. I would never forgive myself if I gave this kidnapper any excuse to..." She couldn't speak the words—couldn't even think the unthinkable!

"If what you're saying is true and this kidnapper has a contact inside the hotel," said Ed, "they'll inform him when your husband starts asking questions, and they might harm Aurelie when that happens."

"You're right," said Odelia. "We need to handle this a different way." She thought for a moment, then seemed to reach a conclusion. "I think we need to think outside the box here, Regarda. Will you trust me to try out a few things?"

She glanced up at Regarda, and the latter could see that the young woman's eyes were filled with gentle concern for her plight. For some reason she trusted her. "Yes," she said. "Please do what you can to get my baby back."

"We've been trying to raise the money," said Ed. "But it's not easy. We're not rich, and fifty thousand is a lot."

"Has the kidnapper been in touch again after the first message?" asked Odelia.

Both Regarda and her son shook their head. "No, he hasn't," said Regarda. "Is that odd?" Fear struck her heart. "Is that... a bad sign?"

"Not necessarily," said Odelia, placing a reassuring hand on her arm. "They're giving you time to collect the money. But at some point they'll be in touch again to give you instructions for the exchange."

"The exchange?"

"The money for Aurelie. So if you could keep me informed? We need to know what kind of time frame we're dealing with."

"Time frame," said Ed, nodding. "Gotcha."

"Usually these people want to move fast. So I wouldn't be surprised if they contacted you today, demanding an update on the money situation. They might also provide proof of life, and if they don't, I'd demand that they do."

"Proof… of life?" said Regarda, blinking confusedly.

"Proof that Aurelie is still alive, Mom," said Ed gently. "A picture or…" He didn't finish the sentence, but the meaning was clear.

"Oh!" Regarda cried, much stricken as she clasped a hand to her chest. She'd seen the movies where kidnappers cut off toes and fingers and sent them to the family. Horrible movies! "Oh, no! They can't harm my baby—not my Aurelie!"

Odelia took her hand in hers and squeezed it. "I'm going to do everything in my power to get Aurelie back to you safe and sound, Regarda. And if anything should happen to her, God forbid, I can promise you that the kidnapper will pay. You have my word on that."

And Regarda could see that she was sincere.

CHAPTER 18

I would have liked to tell you that our plan of escape was foolproof and a great success, but alas, it was not to be. After what felt like hours, but must have been no more than twenty minutes, the van pulled to a stop, and Dooley and I—and Rufus, of course—were fully alert and ready for action. The bags were dragged from the back of the van, and for a moment we were suspended in the air—or at least dangling over someone's shoulder—presumably Johnny's, as he is the designated muscle man in this two-man outfit.

We heard a door creak open, we entered, and the bags were placed on the floor. After a while, Johnny spoke. "Shouldn't we get those cats out of the bag, Jer?"

"We wait for the boss," was Jerry's terse response.

"It's probably cramped in there. Don't you want to know if they're all right?"

"We wait for the boss," Jerry insisted. "He calls the shots."

"But—"

"We wait for the boss!"

"Yes, Jer."

And so I guess we were going to wait for the boss. And since this mysterious boss took his time, the wait lasted a long time. Much too long in my personal estimation!

"How much longer do we have to wait, Max?" asked Dooley.

"I have no idea, Dooley," I said honestly. Since I wasn't privy to the schedule this boss person kept, I had no way of knowing if we were going to be forced to wait an hour, a day, or even a week. Though probably it wouldn't be that long. After all, the fact that we had been taken probably meant they needed us alive and in good shape so they could trade us in for some hard currency.

"I wonder what they did with the baby," said Rufus, whose bag had been placed right next to ours. "I hope they didn't stuff it into a bag, like they did with us. Babies aren't made to be stuffed into bags. They're very delicate creatures."

"We're delicate creatures," I said, "but that didn't stop them from stuffing us into a bag."

"I know, but babies are extra-delicate. So delicate they might break when you stuff them into a bag. They might choke or something."

"I might choke," I muttered darkly. I didn't like being cooped up inside a burlap bag. It wasn't my idea of fun, to tell you the truth.

"I think babies are probably a lot tougher than you think," said Dooley. "Just look at Grace. She's tough as nails."

"Not exactly tough as nails," I said. "Grace had a delicate phase, too, when she was born. Now she's tougher, but in the beginning she was a delicate little thing."

"She was cute, wasn't she?" said Dooley.

I could have reminded him how he once thought Grace

was the spawn of the devil, but didn't. We had other fish to fry—or bags.

"Maybe we can use our claws to cut our way out of here," I said, and applied my claw to the material we were confined in. "Cut a hole, make it bigger, and then worm our way through. Then once we're out, we can get you out, Rufus."

"I'll chew my way out," Rufus announced. "In fact when we were in that van, I was practicing and I think I've got the hang of it. I'll just keep on chewing and you keep on using those claws."

"We should coordinate our efforts," I told Dooley. "I'll start from the top and you start from the bottom and we'll meet in the middle, how about that?"

"Sounds good to me," said Dooley. "I don't like it here, Max. I want to go home."

"We all want to go home, Dooley," I said. "So let's make it happen."

"Before the boss gets here," Rufus added.

And so for the next couple of minutes, Rufus chewed, and Dooley and I cut, and together we worked our way through the material we were confined in. And we probably would have succeeded, if that boss—whoever he was—hadn't arrived on the scene before we were well and truly done.

The door opened and footsteps could be heard. Then the door slammed and Jerry said in obsequious tones, "Boss. We got them right here. And we found a baby, too."

"A baby?" said the boss, who turned out to be a man. Which shouldn't have come as a surprise, since statistically men are more prone to criminal behavior than women, apparently. "What do you mean, a baby? Did I tell you to go out and kidnap babies?"

"It just happened to be crawling around where we

found the cats," Jerry explained, sounding ill at ease. This boss person must be some tough guy, if Jerry was as scared of him as he sounded.

"So let me get this straight. I tell you to snatch a couple of pets, and instead you grab a baby."

"Not instead, also," Jerry said.

"Four for the price of three, boss," said Johnny. "Which is a pretty good deal."

"Plus, people like babies," said Jerry. "They'll pay good money to get it back."

"Shut up," the boss growled. "And show me that baby." The baby must have been shown, for the next thing this boss man said was, "Better drop it off at the nearest hospital. I have no need for a baby. It doesn't fit in with my plans."

"But—"

"Get rid of it, I said! Now where's this dog?"

"It's a big one," said Jerry.

"And a mean one," Johnny added. "A big, mean dog."

"I'm not mean!" said Rufus, greatly insulted. "I'm very sweet—everybody says so. In fact I haven't bitten a single person in my entire life. Okay, so I snap at the mailman's ankles from time to time, but that's simply out of respect for a time-honored tradition. Every dog does that. It's part of our DNA."

"Is that the dog?" asked the boss. "You're right. He sounds mean."

"Oh, he is," Jerry assured the man. "We had a lot of trouble getting him into the bag. He put up a real fight, but in the end we got him, didn't we, Johnny?"

"And you're sure you got the right one?"

"Absolutely, boss. We're professionals."

"Better put a muzzle on him. We don't want no accidents."

"Oh, for sure, boss," said Jerry, sounding pleased. "For sure."

"They want to put a muzzle on me!" Rufus lamented. "A muzzle! Never in my worst nightmare could I have imagined to be treated like this!"

"It'll be all right," I said. "We'll get out of here one way or another. And then we can put a muzzle on these bozos instead."

The prospect pleased our furry friend, for he said, "Thanks, Max. You're a real pal."

"How are we going to get out of here, Max?" asked Dooley. "And how are we going to put that muzzle on these people?"

"I have no idea, Dooley," I said. "But I'll figure it out." Big words, I know, but I had to do something to get us out of this predicament. Or pretty soon they'd put a muzzle on me, too!

CHAPTER 19

Harriet and Brutus welcomed the arrival of Marge and Gran with mixed emotions. It meant they were going home, which was a good thing, but it also meant they were leaving Scarlett's cozy apartment, which wasn't such a good thing, since Scarlett had proven to be adept at spoiling them rotten. In the short time they'd been there, already they'd tasted liver pâté, some gourmet nuggets in the most delicious sauce, and the tastiest chicken filet Brutus had ever sampled.

"If this keeps up they'll be able to roll me out of here," he told Harriet, patting his belly. He was lying on his back on the couch and feeling extremely mellow.

"If this keeps up I'm going to ask Scarlett to adopt us," said Harriet.

They loved their humans, no doubt about it, but they might be induced to love Scarlett just a little bit more. The woman had a way with cats that was delightful.

"I think I'm in love," said Harriet therefore when Scarlett opened another packet of something delicious. "I didn't even know humans like her existed."

"I didn't know she had it in her," Brutus agreed. In all the time they'd known Gran's friend, they hadn't looked upon her as a cat person, but she most definitely was. "She can catsit us any time. Any time at all."

"Or adopt us," said Harriet.

But then the doorbell rang and Marge and Gran walked in and spoiled the fun. Plain old kibble and plain old wet food would be on the menu tonight, not this gourmet meal Scarlett had supplied.

"Too bad," Brutus whispered.

"I never thought I'd say this," Harriet whispered back, "but I don't want to go home!"

They both giggled like naughty kids, and even Grace joined in the fun.

"I always have a great time when I'm over at Auntie Scarlett's," she revealed. "She lets me watch television all day long!"

Okay, so maybe that was too much, Brutus thought. Too much television will rot your brain, after all, or so someone had told him once. But it was obvious that if a popularity contest was held at that moment Scarlett would win hands down—with votes cast by infant and cats alike!

"Oh, there you are," said Marge as she spotted Harriet and Brutus. "Did you know that Odelia has been looking for you everywhere?"

"Define 'everywhere,'" said Harriet.

"Yeah, we've been right here all this time," said Brutus.

"Where are Max and Dooley?" asked Gran. "We need them."

"Last time we saw them they were heading into the field behind the backyard," said Harriet. "Why? What do you need them for?"

"A baby has gone missing," said Marge. "In that same field. And we were hoping Max could help us find it."

"Oh, we know all about that," said Harriet. "In fact we're already on the case. What Max can do, we can do better. Isn't that right, snookums?"

"Absolutely," Brutus agreed. "We came here to ask Grace to help us find that baby, since we all know that finding babies is a baby's job."

"Please leave me out of this," said Grace with an eye roll.

"Okay, so maybe we were wrong about that," Harriet amended her partner's statement. "But we have a plan, haven't we, sparky star?"

"We have?" asked Brutus. But when Harriet made frantic signals with her eyes, he quickly changed that into, "We do! Of course we do. A great plan!"

"What plan?" asked Marge. "And how do you know about this missing baby?"

And so Brutus told her all about their meeting with Jackie's parents, and how they had done everything in their power to find the baby, but so far hadn't succeeded—which didn't mean anything.

"We'll find that baby," Harriet assured their humans. "Trust me."

"Mh," said Marge, displaying an appalling lack of faith in the detecting qualities of her cats. "So where is Max? And Dooley?"

Brutus shrugged. These continuous references to Max and Dooley irked him, as they clearly irked Harriet. "Probably taking a nap," he finally said.

"Last time we saw them they were going to catch some burglars," said Harriet.

"Burglars? What burglars?" asked Gran.

But before they could supply the answer, Marge clapped her hands. "Okay, let's go," she said. The librarian was one of those people who liked decisive action. "Not you, Grace. Could you hang onto her for just a couple of hours more, Scarlett? We're faced with something of an emergency, I'm afraid."

"I know. A missing baby, huh?" said Scarlett. "That's terrible."

"Not just a missing baby. Someone kidnapped a cat this morning."

"Kidnapped a cat!" Harriet cried. "But who? Where? And why!"

And as Marge and Gran filled them in on the kidnapped cat situation, Brutus shook a weary head. "What's happening in this town? First a missing baby, now a kidnapped cat. And don't even get me started on those burglars Max said he saw."

This time Marge gave them a look of alarm. "Burglars? What burglars?"

"That's what I said!" said Gran.

"Max told us he saw two crooks attaching cameras to the back fence," Harriet explained. "Johnny Carew and Jerry Vale. He said they looked as if they were up to a lot of no good. He also said they received instructions from someone they called 'boss.' Max thought he must be some local crime boss."

Marge and Gran shared a look of concern. "I thought those two finally turned their back on crime?" said Gran.

"Maybe they did," said Marge. "Maybe it's just a coincidence."

"I don't believe in coincidences," Gran announced, and all of a sudden turned pensive. "If only we knew where Max was!"

CHAPTER 20

Jack Sanders was reading his paper, seated on his sofa, when his wife Julia called his attention to some strange goings-on in their street. Julia had a habit of standing in front of the window and keeping a close eye on everything that went on in their little corner of the world. Jack himself, a retired roofer, wasn't all that bothered, but he had to admit life outside their window could be most entertaining. Like that time their neighbor had bought an RV to go traveling with his wife, and had managed to get it stuck in his driveway. Now that was a laugh.

"This is the third time I've seen these people," said Julia. "These strange men with their bags over their shoulders. They keep going back and forth to that van of theirs with their bags. Now I do wonder what they're up to, Jack."

"Are you sure it's not Santa Claus?" asked Jack without looking up from his paper.

"Don't be silly. There's two of them, and they don't look like Santa to me. One is big and looks like a gangster, and the other is short and thin and looks like a rat."

"A rat, huh? Don't tell him to his face, darling. He might bite." He chuckled at his little joke, but his wife wasn't laughing.

"Will you get over here and take a look, Jack Sanders? This is your neighborhood, too, and if it goes to the dogs, it affects us all."

With a deep sigh, he put down his paper and got up from his comfy sofa. "Now what's the big emergency?" he said as he joined his wife at the window, both safely hidden behind their net curtains.

"They just carried a bunch of bags into that van over there," said Julia. "And now they're getting in themselves. And driving off."

"You don't have to give me a running commentary of something I can see with my own two eyes," he said. "So what if they put bags into their van? Maybe they're gardeners and those bags are filled with manure. Or maybe they're floorers, or carpenters—or whatever."

"And I think they look like crooks," his wife insisted. "And that's what I'm going to tell Vesta."

"Not Vesta again," Jack groaned.

"Yes, Vesta. At least someone in this neighborhood watches out for us."

"I thought she quit that neighborhood watch nonsense? Her and that kooky friend of hers?"

"Scarlett Canyon," said Julia as she put her phone to her ear. "And it's not just them. Father Reilly and Wilbur Vickery are also members of the watch. And if you had any sense of responsibility you'd join them, too," she admonished him sternly. But as he opened his mouth for a snappy retort, the call connected and she plastered an ingratiating smile onto her face. "Vesta! It's Julia. Julia Sanders. The most suspicious characters have moved in next door, and they're up to something. Yes, very suspicious behavior. They're hauling bags to and from their van. Yes, bags!"

* * *

VESTA PUT HER PHONE AWAY. "That was Julia Sanders," she said. "She just told me that two men answering to the description of Johnny Vale and Jerry Carew have moved next door to her, and she just saw them dragging bags to and from their van."

Marge arched a meaningful eyebrow. "Bags?"

"Bags. And she couldn't be absolutely sure, but she thinks she saw one of the bags move."

"You don't think..."

"I'm not sure what to think. But let's examine the facts, Marge: Max saw those two crooks put cameras on our back fence. A cat has been kidnapped. A baby has gone missing. And Max and Dooley are nowhere to be found. Isn't it possible that Max caught these fellas in the act of grabbing that baby, or stealing that cat, and so they took him, too? Him and Dooley? It would explain those bags."

"Oh, dear," said Marge, shaking her head in dismay. "You really think Jackie was kidnapped, do you?"

"It would explain why the Pearces can't find her."

They were home, where a sort of command center had been set up. Chase had arrived, and also Alec, and they were going over their plan of campaign. Since the field that stretched out behind the house was pretty big, they had decided to rope in some of the neighbors, or at least as many neighbors as they could find, and soon the Trappers arrived, Ted and Marcie, and also Kurt Mayfield. And when Blake Carrington himself walked in, who owned the field, they had a nice group who could comb that field and find Jackie.

Vesta had relayed her suspicions to her son, but Alec wasn't buying it. "Now why would Vale and Carew kidnap a baby? That doesn't make sense. And besides, the Pearces haven't received any ransom demand."

"Max told Harriet and Brutus they're working for a third party," Vesta explained. "So maybe this third party is in the kidnapping business? And that ransom demand will come in at some point tonight? I wouldn't rule it out, Alec. Nor would I rule out that our cats have also been taken."

"Max and Dooley haven't been taken," said Alec. "They're much too clever to allow themselves to be grabbed by two bumbling fools like Vale and Carew."

"So where are they? And why hasn't anybody seen them since this morning?"

"They're out there… somewhere," said Alec, gesturing vaguely in the direction of town. "Doing what they always do, which is sticking their noses where they don't belong. And now please don't bother me again with these wild ideas of yours, will you, Ma? I have a baby to find, and preferably before nightfall. So if you don't mind…"

Vesta knew when she wasn't wanted, so she retreated gracefully. Or at least as gracefully as was her wont. "You're an ass, Alec Lip," she snapped. She turned to her daughter. "We need to find Max and Dooley. And I'm pretty sure that when we do, we'll find that missing baby—and that cat."

CHAPTER 21

Chase watched on as Alec introduced Blake to the rest of those present. Most of them didn't need the introduction since Blake was a well-known figure in Hampton Cove. They were all familiar with the tragedy that had befallen him many years ago, when his son had been killed during an illegal street race. Blake had never fully recovered. But since it was his land Jackie had disappeared on, Alec had asked him to attend the meeting.

Chase shook Blake's hand, and was surprised by how firm it was. The man looked like an older version of Chase's own father-in-law Tex, with a shock of white hair and a weather-beaten face, and he could see he must have been a very handsome man. He was still handsome, though there was also something sad about him.

"Terrible news about this missing child," said Blake. "And Alec tells me she disappeared on my land?"

Chase nodded. "The Pearces live a couple of houses down from here, and Jackie must have escaped through the little back gate and into your field. They looked for her everywhere but so far no luck."

"She could be anywhere by now," said Blake as he rubbed his chin thoughtfully. "Odd that no one has seen her, though. You'd expect people to pay attention when they see an unattended child wandering around."

"You would," said Chase with a sigh. "Only nowadays people are often so engrossed in their phones and their own business they don't notice much at all of the world around them. It's the darnedest thing."

"True," Blake agreed. "Just now, driving over here, I almost hit a woman suddenly crossing the road, staring at her phone. She hadn't seen me until I practically hit her. Dangerous trend."

"It is," Chase said. "So we have permission to search your land, sir?"

"Of course. And please sign me up as one of your volunteers. I want this baby found just as badly as her parents do."

"Thank you, sir," said Chase. "I know how important the field is to you—and the shrine, of course."

Blake winced. "I wouldn't exactly call it a shrine, though I guess to some extent it is exactly that." After his son died, Blake decided to keep everything exactly as it was, as a testament to his son's life. Over the years weeds and encroaching plant life had caused the spot to become overgrown, and nowadays it was hard to imagine that once it had been destined to be turned into another row of fine family homes.

"Okay, let's begin," said Alec, clapping his hands. The house had filled up nicely, with plenty of volunteers eager to lend a helping hand. And as Alec explained the grid search system, Chase saw how his father-in-law stood eyeing their neighbor Ted with unveiled hostility. Uh-oh, he thought. Trouble ahead!

* * *

Tex had sidled up to his neighbor, and now whispered, "I know what you did, Ted."

"And what did I do, Tex?" asked Ted.

"You installed cameras on my back fence so you can spy on me."

"Now why would I go and do that?" said Ted, and he looked genuinely surprised by this accusation.

"To make sure I'm not home when you're destroying my gnomes!"

"That wasn't me! I told you this morning. That wasn't me, Tex!"

"Liar."

"Now, Tex. That's not very neighborly of you, is it?"

"It's not very neighborly to destroy my gnomes."

"I'm telling you: it wasn't me!"

"I know a big, fat liar when I see one, Ted, and you're it."

"Look, I know you don't like me very much, Tex, because my gnome collection is bigger and nicer than yours—"

"You said *my* collection was nicer!"

"I lied, all right! But that's still no reason to treat me with this hostility. I did *not* destroy your gnomes. And I did *not* install any cameras on your back fence!"

Tex stared at the man, but Ted stared right back, and didn't relent. Either the man was an expert liar, or he was telling the truth.

"But… if you didn't put those cameras there, then who did?"

"The real saboteur, no doubt," Ted said, and that actually made sense. "Someone is out to destroy your collection, Tex, and it's not me." He placed a hand on his shoulder. "As your neighbor, and your friend, I respect you too much to do a thing like that, you know that."

"Mh," said Tex without much excitement. "I guess."

"Spoken like a true gnome collector," said Ted with a big grin. "Now all we have to do is find out who really put those cameras there."

"Oh, but we know who put those cameras there," said Chase, who had approached the dueling duo. "It was Vale and Carew. Two career criminals. We have a witness who saw them do it this morning."

Tex's eyes went wide. "But then why did nobody tell me!"

"This morning?" said Ted. "But Tex's gnomes were vandalized last night."

"Norbert was attacked last night, but Jackson Brown was attacked three days ago," said Tex. "So if Vale and Carew put those cameras up this morning, it couldn't have been them." He turned back to Ted and eyed him with suspicion.

But Ted held up his arms. "I didn't do it—I swear!"

"All right, Ted," said Chase, clapping the other man on the back. "We believe you. Don't we, Dad?" And he gave his father-in-law an intent look. "Don't we?"

"Mh," Tex repeated. He still wasn't too sure he believed that Ted was telling the truth. The man was an accountant, and accountants are known to fiddle. Fiddle with their tax returns, fiddle with expense reports, bills—and gnomes!

"Okay, so once this whole missing baby business is dealt with, I'll take a closer look at this vandalism thing," Chase suggested. "How does that sound, Dad?"

"Good," Tex said without much conviction. Chase was a busy man, and once this baby was found, there would be some other emergency, and then another, and his poor gnomes would always take a back seat to the murderers and burglars and other criminal elements of this world.

"I promise, Dad," said Chase emphatically as he leaned in.

Tex cracked a smile at his son-in-law. "All right, fine. You look for those vandals, and I'll remove those cameras."

"Or you could leave them," Ted suggested. "And take them over."

"Take them over? What do you mean, take them over?"

"Vesta knows this computer geek, doesn't she? So why don't you ask him to take control of those cameras? That way you don't have to buy them yourself and you can still keep an eye on your backyard."

"Is that even possible?" asked Tex, who was a complete computer illiterate.

"I think it is," said Ted. "In fact I might ask this whizz kid of yours to install a couple of cameras for me, too. Just to be on the safe side."

"You don't have to install any cameras, Ted," said Chase. "Vale and Carew put cameras all over the place. Your back fence, Dad's, ours, Mayfield's... I don't know what they're up to, but I intend to find out."

"So they *are* targeting me," said Ted quietly. He looked stunned.

Tex eyed his neighbor closely, but couldn't detect a sign of deceit.

Ted suddenly held out his hand. "I know we don't always see eye to eye, neighbor, but when it comes to making sure our gnomes are safe from vandalism, I believe now is the time to join forces. Work together as a team."

"Mh," said Tex for the third time since engaging his neighbor in conversation. "So who's to say *you* aren't the evil mastermind behind Vale and Carew, Ted?"

"But why would I put cameras on my own back fence!"

"To avert suspicion, of course! A classic move!"

"If that's what you think, I have nothing more to say to you, Tex," said Ted haughtily, and started to walk away.

"I'm keeping an eye on you, Ted!" Tex cried.

Ted wheeled around. "And I'm keeping an eye on you!"

CHAPTER 22

"'Where is Max? Where is Max?'" Harriet mimicked annoyedly. "As if Max is the only cat who gets things done around here. What about us, huh?"

"Yeah, what about us?" Brutus chimed in.

The not-so-happy couple was seated under their favorite rose bush in Odelia's backyard, discussing recent events, and more specifically Max and Dooley's so-called disappearance.

"I don't believe for one second that Max went missing," said Harriet. "He's probably out there somewhere detecting something. Solving some murder or hot on the trail of some major criminal."

"Absolutely," said Brutus.

"But instead of asking us to find Jackie, all they can say is, 'Where is Max! Oh, if only Max was here!' It makes me sick, sugar pants."

"And me," Brutus concurred.

"I mean, don't get me wrong. I love Max. He's one of

my dearest, dearest friends, but he's not a superhero. He's just a cat—like us!"

"Of course he is. Just a cat," Brutus echoed.

"And if he's gone missing, so be it. There are other feline sleuths who can take over from him." She tapped her chest. "*Moi*!"

"And *moi*," Brutus added. He cleared his throat. "It is odd, though, isn't it, that Max and Dooley haven't been seen for hours? I mean, Shanille hasn't seen them, or Kingman, or even Buster."

"He's out there detecting, pumpkin! And you know Max. Once he sniffs out a clue, he's like a dog with a bone. He's off and running! No stopping him!"

"Yeah, I guess." Brutus was quiet for a moment, and seemed on the verge of saying something, but then thought better of it.

"Just spit it out," said Harriet finally.

"I don't know. I'm still a little worried, aren't you?"

"No, I'm not. Max can take care of himself. He doesn't need us to worry about him. And neither does Dooley." They shared a look, then she added, "Okay, so it is a little worrying that neither Kingman or Shanille know where he is. Those two always know everything."

"They do know everything."

"I come in peace!" suddenly a voice piped up somewhere close by. "Please don't take a swipe at me!"

Harriet looked up, and saw that a butterfly had approached. She recognized it as the same butterfly who had soiled her perfect fur that morning. "Don't come near me," she said. "I'm warning you."

"Oh, trust me, I won't come anywhere near you," said the butterfly. "In fact if I had any other choice I wouldn't even come this close to you, you butterfly hater."

"I'm not a butterfly hater," said Harriet. "I just don't like it when you put your stuff on me."

"That stuff is called pollen," said the butterfly, "and it's very good for your complexion. But whatever."

"Just tell us what you want," said Harriet, who wasn't in the mood to nurse the delicate ego of a butterfly on top of everything else she had to deal with.

"Max and Dooley are your friends, right? So I saw them out in the field earlier, accompanied by Rufus and Fifi. The four of them were watching a baby who must have wandered away from its home and got lost. So they asked me to go look for its parents, which I did. Unfortunately I couldn't find them, but when I returned to deliver this message, they were gone."

"Who was gone?" asked Harriet with a frown.

"All of them! Max, Dooley, Fifi and Rufus. And the baby. Gone."

"So where did they go?"

"Beats me. Haven't seen them since," said the butterfly.

"Listen… what's your name?"

"Flora."

"Listen, Flora. This is not the time to play games. Did you actually see Max and Dooley with a baby?"

"Absolutely."

"And next thing you know they were gone."

"They were gone. Vanished without a trace. I did see a van pull away from the curb on the other side of the field. Those two fellas were in that van. The ones who've been hanging out here the last couple of days installing those cameras."

"Johnny and Jerry," said Brutus immediately.

"You don't think…" said Harriet.

"Yes, I do," said Brutus.

"But they wouldn't…"

"Yes, they would."

"But why?"

Brutus quirked a whisker at her.

"Okay, dumb question. What I meant was: they know that Max and Dooley belong to Odelia and Marge—and they know us. They like our family. They wouldn't harm us, would they?"

"I don't know, starfish. But if Flora says they were there, it's an awfully big coincidence, isn't it?"

"I know." She heaved a deep sigh. "The plot thickens."

"That, it does," Brutus agreed.

"Okay, so who are these guys?" asked Flora, her curiosity piqued.

"Two crooks," said Harriet. "With a record as long as my paw."

"Try two paws," said Brutus. "Or even four."

"You have to find them," said Flora. "Cause as it stands, I think it's very likely that they took Max, Dooley, Rufus, Fifi—and the baby."

"What's all this about me being taken?" suddenly another voice piped up. It was Fifi, and contrary to popular opinion, she clearly had not been taken by anyone, since she was staring right at them.

"Fifi!" Harriet cried. "You're okay!"

"Of course I'm okay," said Fifi. "Why wouldn't I be?"

"But… that butterfly over there—"

"Flora," Flora said.

"Flora over there says you were kidnapped, along with Max, Dooley and Rufus."

"And the baby," Flora added.

"Kidnapped? But I just saw them," said Fifi.

"And now they're gone," said Flora. "Vanished. Poof."

"But…" Fifi gulped a little. "But I left them. I didn't

want to be responsible for a baby so I left them—and now they're gone?"

"They may have been kidnapped," said Brutus.

"Oh, dear God, no!" said Fifi, and became extremely upset all of a sudden. "I should never have left them. What did I do!"

"If you wouldn't have left, you would have been taken, too," Brutus said.

But his words couldn't console the little Yorkie. "I left my friends in their hour of need. I'm the worst friend in the world!" she cried. "The absolute worst!"

"Look, it's no use crying over spilled milk," said Harriet, who might be something of a drama queen herself but didn't condone the same behavior in others. "What's done is done. And besides, you couldn't have known they were going to be taken, could you? So let's focus on what needs to be done to get them back."

"But I left them! I left them high and dry!"

"Fifi! Focus!" said Harriet, and would have snapped her fingers if she could. Instead she gave the little doggie a light slap across the face, causing her to snap out of whatever episode she was going through. "What can you tell us that will help us find our friends?"

Fifi blinked and tried to focus. "Not much. There was a baby, and we were going to watch it until Flora returned with its parents. But I got bored and so I left. Oh, what did I do!"

"Fifi!"

"I don't know what happened, all right! I left them. I abandoned my friends!"

"We were actually there," said Harriet. "We heard a terrible scream and so we went looking for Max and Dooley. But all we found was this Maggie Pearce person thrashing about and screaming like some kind of maniac."

"Why was she screaming?" asked Flora.

"She was looking for her baby," Brutus said. "And so was her husband."

"I wonder what happened out there," said Flora. "Sounds like a real mystery."

"Okay, none of this matters," said Harriet, taking control. "All we have to do now—the only thing we should focus on from now on—is to find our friends."

"And the baby," Flora supplied helpfully.

CHAPTER 23

"I'm getting seasick," said Dooley.

"Me, too," I admitted.

We were getting schlepped all over the place. In the van, out of the van, in the van… And all the while they kept us in those terrible bags.

"Have you managed to bite through your bag, Rufus?" I asked.

"I don't get the chance!" Rufus lamented. "They keep shifting us around. I have managed to tear a tiny hole, and at least I can see the inside of the van, but it's nowhere big enough to crawl through, you guys."

"Same here," I grumbled. It was tough going with this material, which was pretty durable. I'd managed to create a tiny tear, and could look into the van, but that was about it.

"I think I'm going to be sick," said Dooley.

"Please don't," I told my friend.

"Who's driving?" asked Rufus. "Because whoever it is, you can tell him from me that he's a terrible driver."

"I'll tell him when I get the chance," I said dryly. "Okay, so same message, people. The moment they untie this bag, we escape, all right? We scratch, we claw and we bite our way out, and we don't care who gets hurt."

"I hope we don't get hurt," said Dooley.

"No, that's exactly the point," I said. "We escape to prevent us from getting hurt."

"I wonder where that baby is," said Rufus. "They said they were going to drop it off at the hospital, so let's hope they weren't kidding."

"That man, whoever he is, didn't sound like he was a great kidder," I said.

"Did you recognize his voice?" asked Rufus. "Did he sound familiar to you?"

"No, he didn't," I said. I'd been thinking the same thing. We knew a lot of people in Hampton Cove, but I didn't think we'd ever met this particular person before. I would have recognized his voice.

"He must be an associate of those two criminals," said Rufus.

The van had come to a stop again, and the engine was soon switched off. Sounds of voices could be heard, and next thing we knew the side door of the van was pulled open and strong hands grabbed the bag and hoisted us up —again!

"I'm going to be sick, Max!" Dooley cried. And true enough, this time he actually was sick.

"Did you hear that, Jer?" Johnny asked. "It sounded like someone is upchucking something." A pause, then: "My ass is wet. Why is my ass wet, Jer?"

"Just hurry up, will you?" said Jerry irritably. "Don't drag your feet."

"I'm not dragging my feet but my ass is wet all of a sudden."

The bag was put down as Johnny presumably tried to look at his own ass. I glanced through the little tear in the bag and saw how the big guy was patting his butt and came away with some of Dooley's vomit. He smelled his hand and made a face.

"Jer! Someone upchucked against my butt!"

"Oh, will you shut up and grab that bag!"

"But it's true! Must be one of the cats, Jer!"

"I'm sorry," said Dooley. "I couldn't hold it in any longer."

"Are you all right, buddy?" I asked, concerned about my friend.

"I'm fine now," said Dooley. "It's the motion of the van, Max."

"I know. Let's hope we're done with that van now."

"It's true, though, Jer," said Johnny as he picked up our bag again. "Someone threw up against my butt. It must be the cats. I didn't even know cats could throw up. Imagine if that dog throws up, too. It's going to make a big mess, Jer."

But then we were inside a house, and were unceremoniously dumped in the corner of a room. Johnny left, the door was locked and bolted and then we were alone. Or at least I thought we were alone, until a soft voice piped up, "Is anybody in there, please?"

"Who are you?" I asked, as I tried to ascertain who the voice belonged to. But unfortunately the tear was facing the wall. Not a very nice wall, either, but covered in peeling paint.

"My name is Aurelie," said the voice, "and I was taken this morning from my hotel room. Who are you?"

"My name is Max," I said. "And my friend Dooley is also in here."

"Hi," said Dooley. "I threw up before, so if I smell bad please don't hold it against me. It was the van and the bad driving."

"So you were taken, too, were you?" said Aurelie. "Oh, this is such a nightmare."

"Are you also inside a bag?" I asked.

"Oh, no," said Aurelie. "And neither are you."

"What do you mean? We're tied up in here."

"No, you're not. That fat man removed the tie."

And when I pushed up, I immediately discovered that she was right. Johnny must have quickly removed the tie without either of us noticing. So much for our amazing escape plan!

I stepped out of the bag, and found myself in a small room, a smallish fluffy sort of cat staring back at me with a sad look in her eyes. "There's only one litter box, and it's not even clean," she said.

"That's all right," I said. "I'm not planning on being in here long."

"Oh, so you know how to get out of here?" she asked, hope rising in her voice.

"Not exactly, but I'm going to find out."

"Oh," she said, and deflated somewhat.

Dooley had joined us, and even though he looked as if he'd been through the wars, he still looked happy to be rid of the bag. "Fresh air!" he said. "So nice!"

"It's not very fresh, though," said Aurelie. "In fact the air is pretty bad in here."

"Where is Rufus?" I asked.

"Who's Rufus?" asked Aurelie.

"Our friend," I explained. "We were all taken together, and also a baby named Jackie. But it's possible that they released the baby."

"A baby!" Aurelie cried. "Who would take a baby!"

"Yeah, I think they took the baby by accident," I said.

"I've seen the man who took me," said Aurelie. "He

didn't look like a criminal. In fact when I first saw him I thought he looked nice."

"You actually saw this man's face?" I said.

Aurelie nodded. "When he came into my hotel room."

"What did he look like?" I asked.

"Well, young, and handsome. Like a movie star."

"So it wasn't Johnny and it wasn't Jerry," I said. Neither of them look like movie stars. At least not the movie stars I know. Maybe Aurelie had a different idea in mind about what constitutes a movie star, of course.

"Okay, so I need to know what happened to Rufus," I said. "And I need to know how to get out of this place."

Dooley had settled down next to Aurelie and the two of them were chatting amiably while I investigated the room for any means of egress. "We're from Berlin, that's in Maryland," said Aurelie, "and my human is named Regarda Cooper. Her son was going to get married to a woman named Sara last month, but at the last minute she had a change of heart and decided to skip the wedding. Unfortunately Ed was already standing at the altar waiting for her, and so was the priest and all the guests. It was a big to-do and Ed's cousin Danny filmed everything and put it on YouTube and the video went viral and now Ed is famous but he's also very sad. And since he had already paid for the honeymoon Regarda suggested she join him and so here we are."

"What a story," Dooley gushed. "So do you think this Sara person kidnapped you? To get back at her fiancé?"

Aurelie regarded him strangely. "Now why would she do that? He's the one who's mad at her, not the other way around."

"So why did she decide to call off the wedding? Ed must have done something to upset her."

"It's her heart. Someone took out the old one and put in

a new one, and somehow she stopped loving Ed. Ed tried calling, he tried texting, but she's blocking him. And no other explanations. So except for the heart part we don't know why she called it off. Which is why Ed finds it so hard to get over her."

"He needs closure," I said as I inspected a crack in the wall. "He needs to know what happened so he can put the whole thing behind him and move on."

"That's what Regarda keeps telling him, and why she's so mad at Sara for standing him up like that and refusing to explain." She smiled at Dooley. "But I'm pretty sure she has nothing to do with this kidnapping, Dooley."

"Well, I just thought she might be angry with Ed," said Dooley, "for some unknown reason, so angry she called off the wedding, and then organized this kidnapping to get back at Ed for whatever reason."

"I doubt it," said Aurelie. "Ed is just about the nicest man on the planet. He's probably too nice and too sweet. At least that's what I think." She glanced in my direction. "Any luck finding an escape route, Max?"

"Nope," I said. "Not yet. But I won't give up, Aurelie. We *are* getting out of here. It's just a matter of time."

And patience. And figuring out a plan!

CHAPTER 24

Ed had to admit he wasn't exactly feeling on top of the world. But then he hadn't felt on top of the world since his wedding had descended into a scene from a farce. If someone had started a food fight and he'd received the wedding cake in his face it wouldn't have looked out of place in that church at that moment—possibly the worst moment of his life.

And now Aurelie had been kidnapped and he desperately needed to get back in touch with Sara—the last person in the world he wanted to talk to right now. Not only had she broken his heart and made a fool of him in front of his entire family and circle of friends, but she had refused to tell him why. She had ghosted him, and had induced the rest of her family to ghost him, too.

It just seemed cruel beyond compare.

Which is why he was a little shocked when he read her message. 'I'll ship you the engagement ring ASAP if you text me the address.'

A wealth of emotion raced through him as he read the

message for the dozenth time. It wasn't much, simply a practical message, but knowing that this was the first time she had contacted him since that botched wedding meant something.

He quickly texted her the address, hesitated for a moment on whether to add a more personal message, then decided against it and hit the send icon. He wasn't going to be drawn into recriminations or accusations anymore. Those days were behind him now. He still wanted to know why she had dumped him, but he knew she'd never tell, and that he had to accept the unacceptable if he was ever going to be able to move on with his life the way she had moved on with hers.

"She's sending the ring," he told his mother. "Sara texted me and she's sending the ring."

Mom stuck her head out of the bathroom where she had been washing her face. "No way!"

"Yes!"

"Oh, Ed, you're making me so happy right now. That means we might be able to make it."

"Has the kidnapper been in touch yet?"

"Not yet, but it's early days. Odelia said it could take a little while. They want us to sweat."

Just then, her phone chimed and they both shared a look of surprise. Then Mom dove for her phone, which was on the bed, and grabbed it. She gasped in shock when she saw the message.

"What is it?" asked Ed. "Is it them?"

Mom nodded, and pressed the phone to her chest. "What did Odelia call it? Sign of life?"

"Proof of life," said Ed.

"Well, here it is," said Mom, and showed him the message. It was a picture of Aurelie next to today's newspaper, with as a backdrop an ugly-looking wall.

"My darling looks terrible!" Mom moaned. "Doesn't she look terrible?"

"She has looked happier," Ed conceded. "But at least she's alive, Mom. And they haven't hurt her, I don't think."

"No, she seems fine," Mom agreed. She squeezed her eyes closed. "It's a terrible thing to say but I couldn't help remembering those movies where they cut off a kidnapped person's finger and send it to the family." She looked up at her son. "I really thought for a moment they were going to cut off… Aurelie's ear!"

"Oh, Mom," said Ed, and gave his mother a hug. "Don't think like that. You'll drive yourself crazy."

"I know, but I can't help it!"

"At least now you know she's alive."

"But no other message. Nothing."

"Patience," he said, even though he had a pretty hard time being patient himself. "We just need to be patient and trust Odelia."

"You're right. She knows what she's doing, doesn't she?"

"I'm sure she does." At least he hoped she did!

Suddenly his phone dinged and he checked it. Much surprised he saw that it was Sara. 'Any news about Aurelie? How is your mom holding up? I'm so sorry about what happened.'

He gaped at his phone. Was she referring to the wedding? No, of course not. She was referring to the kidnapping.

"Sara again?" asked Mom as she tried to read the message.

He nodded. "She wants to know how you're holding up."

"Badly," said Mom. "No thanks to her."

"Sara isn't the one who took Aurelie, Mom."

"No, but she's the one who dumped you at the altar,

making me join you on your honeymoon, and Aurelie to be taken. So actually this is Sara's fault. All of it. And you better tell her that," she said as she tapped Ed's phone.

"I'm not telling her anything of the kind," said Ed.

"Well, you should," Mom grumbled as she crossed her arms in front of her chest.

But instead Ed wrote, 'Mom isn't doing so well. Just heard from kidnapper and received proof of life so at least we know Aurelie is alive.' He clicked 'Send' and waited. He saw that Sara was typing. Three dots appeared for a moment, then disappeared again. He waited some more, but no more dots appeared. Apparently Sara had changed her mind about whatever she wanted to write.

* * *

"OKAY, SO YOU KNOW THE PLAN?" asked Odelia.

"Yes, we know the plan," said Harriet, and Odelia just knew the prissy Persian was rolling her eyes.

That's why she preferred to work with Max. Max never rolled his eyes when they went on a mission together, and he never needed to be told the plan since he usually came up with a better one.

It had taken Odelia a while to find Harriet and Brutus, who had been holed up underneath the rose bush again, talking to a butterfly. The butterfly had told them about how the cats had gone missing, along with Rufus and Jackie, and how she had seen Vale and Carew step into their van, parked on the next street. So now it would appear that Max and Dooley had been kidnapped, too, and so had Rufus and Jackie.

She had relayed the information to her uncle, but he told her Johnny and Jerry weren't in the business of kidnapping either babies, dogs or cats, so her intel was flawed. She had told her husband, and he said he'd look into it. Which meant she was on her own, with only Harriet and Brutus to lean on in the search for Aurelie.

As she saw it, when they found Aurelie, they would find the others, as it was highly unlikely there were two kidnappers active in the same area at the same time.

"Okay, so I'll drop you guys off at the kitchen entrance, and then you're on your own," she said.

"We'll handle it," Brutus assured her. "We're seasoned pros, Odelia. Anything Max can do, we can do better. Isn't that right, buttercup?"

"Absolutely," said Harriet.

Now it was Odelia's turn to roll her eyes. She loved all of her cats equally, but no one could convince her Max wasn't the greatest sleuth she had ever met. He simply had a knack for sniffing out the truth. She didn't know how he did it, but he managed to find the guilty party every time. She just hoped he was all right. But knowing Johnny and Jerry she didn't think they'd let any harm come to her cats. They might be crooks, but they weren't all bad.

She had parked her car in the alley behind the Star Hotel, and opened the door to let Harriet and Brutus out. Both cats slipped from the car, and padded over to the kitchen entrance. For a moment they took cover behind a dumpster, patiently waiting. It didn't take more than five minutes for the back door to open and one of the waiters to step into the alley for a smoke. The moment he stepped out, they walked in, moving quick as a flash and earning Odelia's admiration. How fast they were—and how graceful!

She just hoped they'd get the information she needed, and get it fast enough so they could get the pets and Jackie to safety. And she had sat there for another ten minutes when Chase called.

"I got Vale and Carew's current address from their parole officer and sent a team down there to check. Don't get your hopes up, though. They might not be the smartest tools in the shed, but I don't think they're dumb enough to keep the cats at their official address."

"I talked to Gran, and she tells me a neighbor saw them leave a house on Rutherford Street," said Odelia. "They were dragging bags to and from a van. She and Mom are heading over there now to check it out."

"Rutherford Street? No, that's not the address I got. Grover Street is what the parole officer told me," said Chase. "Though it's possible they gave him a false address, of course. Or maybe they moved again." Then: "Are you sure it's a good idea for your mom and gran to get mixed up in this?"

"Even if I wanted to, there's no stopping them, babe. You know what Gran is like."

"Oh, do I?" he grunted. "I almost feel sorry for those two idiots. When your gran gets her hands on them, there will be hell to pay."

"I still don't get how they got mixed up in this. Kidnapping isn't their usual MO."

"As I see it their only MO is to get up to dumb stuff," said Chase with a touch of acerbity. "Which means this is right up their alley."

"Well, I've got Harriet and Brutus trying to figure out who tipped off the kidnappers. And Mom and Gran going after Johnny and Jerry. So let's hope between us we come up with something good."

"Did I tell you that I broke up an argument between your dad and Ted? Apparently your dad thought that Ted was spying on his gnomes so he could destroy them." Odelia could hear the smile in her husband's voice. "When I told them it was actually Vale and Carew who planted those cameras Tex looked more disappointed than pleased. Though now he thinks Ted is a criminal mastermind."

"Dad hasn't been himself lately," said Odelia. "Ever since he entered that gnome competition he's been on edge."

"I talked to Blake Carrington. Apparently he's also into gnomes—big time. I think this is going to be a case of two dogs fighting over a gnome and the third dog running away with it."

Odelia laughed. "Thanks for that."

"For what?"

"For making me laugh. I needed that."

Chase turned serious again. "We'll find our cats, babe. We will. And once we do, we'll throw the book at the fools who took them."

She smiled. "You said 'our cats.'"

"I did, didn't I? What can I say? I love those fur-balls."

"So do I." Just then, there was a sort of commotion at the kitchen entrance. A man stepped out of the hotel, looking highly irate. He had a cat dangling from each hand, and neatly deposited them on the ground, then quickly returned indoors and slammed the door.

Harriet and Brutus, for it was them, shrugged off the disgrace of being kicked out of the hotel, and slowly pranced over to the car.

"Gotta go, babe," said Odelia. "There's been a development."

"Keep me posted," said Chase curtly.

CHAPTER 25

It wasn't an easy mission, as missions go, and Brutus had his qualms. Then again, they'd told Odelia they were easily as good at this sleuthing thing as Max was, probably even better. So now they had to put their money where their mouth was and deliver. And at first things proceeded just fine: they entered the hotel like absolute pros: undetected and stealthily sneaking into the inner lair where Aurelie's kidnapper's accomplice lurked. The lion's den, so to speak.

"How are we going to find this accomplice?" he asked as they carefully snuck through the kitchen. "We don't even know what he looks like—or she."

"We'll just have to follow our inner detective," said Harriet.

Since Brutus had no idea who this inner detective could possibly be, but didn't want to look foolish in front of his mate, he wisely refrained from comment. He'd heard about the inner child, though he had his doubts whether such a construct existed, but an inner detective? Highly suspect. At least he'd never heard Max mention anything about an inner detective, and Max was probably the ultimate sleuth, whether Harriet wanted to admit it or not.

They'd reached the reception desk, the heart of the hotel, and settled down underneath the desk, hoping to glean some useful information about this possible accomplice of Aurelie's kidnapper.

And as luck would have it, they didn't have long to wait. The two receptionists were chatting, and the topic of conversation just happened to be... Aurelie's kidnapping!

"This is bad," said one receptionist, an unshaven youth who looked as if he was fresh out of high school. "This is so bad."

"What do you mean?" asked the other receptionist, a young woman with freckles and a ponytail. "What are you talking about?"

"The kidnapping, of course," said the youth, whose name was Ben. "It's going to attract all kinds of bad press, and the Star's reputation is going to be shot."

"Kidnapping? What kidnapping?" asked the girl, who was named Susie. "I haven't heard about no kidnapping."

Ben lowered his voice, possibly to avoid being overheard by two nosy cats hiding underneath the desk. "The cat of one of the guests was taken in broad daylight—from her room, if you please! Someone actually walked in here, cool as dammit, went upstairs, managed to open the door and grabbed her cat. Now he's asking fifty thousand smackeroos for the safe return of the animal."

"Who—do you know who the cat belongs to?"

"The Pearces," said Ben, and Brutus thought he could hear the girl utter a little cry of shock. "Why, do you know the Pearces?"

"Not personally," said Susie quickly. "When was this?"

"Oh, this morning," said Ben. "When they were at the beach."

"Oh, God," said Susie in a small voice. "That's so terrible!"

"Yeah, it's pretty bad. Bad for us—bad for the hotel."

"How-how do you know all this?" asked Susie.

"My cousin is a cop. Apparently the woman didn't want to go to the police, so instead she talked to this Odelia Kingsley woman, who's married to Chase Kingsley—the detective? And so my cousin happened to overhear Detective Kingsley discuss the case with Chief Lip. The walls have ears in that precinct."

"Same way they do in here," said Susie, who seemed pensive all of a sudden.

"I know, right?" said Ben. "Last week I was chatting with Francine, one of the maids, and she was complaining about Jacqueline, the head of housekeeping. No more than twenty minutes had passed before Francine was called into Jacqueline's office. Our whole conversation had been passed on to her, and Francine was fired. On the spot!"

"Good thing you weren't fired."

"Well, lucky for us our boss isn't as brutal as Jacqueline."

"No, Boris is the best," Susie agreed.

"Oh, there he is. Quick, pretend you're working. He might be a great boss, but he hates it when people don't pull their weight. Hi, sir!" he said, raising his voice.

"Ben," a voice grunted. "Susie. Quiet day?"

"Oh, no, sir," Ben said. "Busy, busy, busy!"

"Mh. You don't look busy to me. Susie, come along with me. Looks like Ben can handle things by himself for a little while."

"Yes, sir," said Susie, and traipsed after the big boss.

"They're splitting up!" said Brutus. "Who should we trail?"

"Let's follow along," Harriet suggested. "Bosses always

have interesting information to share. And who knows what we'll learn."

And so they followed from a distance as Susie and Boris disappeared into the hotel's inner sanctum. Behind the reception desk a corridor led to a series of offices, and it was one of these offices that Boris and Susie entered. Lucky for them the door was left ajar, and so they had no trouble slipping inside and hiding behind a sizable potted plant that had seen better days and needed watering.

Boris had taken position behind his desk, with Susie taking a seat in front of it. The man steepled his fingers on his blotter and fixed his employee with a stern but fatherly look.

"Why did you do it, Susie?" he asked now.

"Do what, sir?" asked Susie, shuffling a little nervously in her seat.

"Let's not play games, shall we? As the person in charge of reception, I see all, know all and, most importantly, am in a position to do something about it when my people cross the line."

"I don't think I crossed any lines, sir," said Susie, but she sounded scared.

"Come, come," said Boris, and the fatherly tone became more pronounced. "You know as well as I do that the Star Hotel doesn't exactly pay its staff a living wage, Susie. So when members of my staff accept tips from guests in exchange for dubious favors, I turn a blind eye. But kidnapping a guest's precious pet? This is going to bite us in the tush, Susie, you do realize that, don't you?"

"But sir!" said Susie. "You're not seriously suggesting that I had something to do with that!"

"That's exactly what I'm suggesting." The unctuousness of his tone increased, and honey dripped from his words when he said, "You're one of my most talented staff members. You can go places, I've said that from the beginning. But this is grounds for dismissal, Susie, you do understand that, don't you? Not only that, but a formal complaint will have to be filed against you with the police. And when convicted, it will go on your record, and your bright future will be bright no more. In fact you won't find a decent job in the hospitality industry ever again—or anywhere else, for that matter. And that will be the end of a promising career."

Suddenly, Susie buried her face in her hands and burst into tears. Her shoulders were quaking and when she spoke again, it was in sobs. "I didn't know he was going to grab that cat, Boris, I promise!"

"Tell me exactly what happened," Boris said as he dragged a couple of tissues from a dispenser and pressed them into the stricken young woman's hand. "And leave out no detail however slight."

"So I met this guy one night at the Café Baron—that's a popular bar."

"I know what the Café Baron is," Boris assured her.

"He said his name was Jim, and he was good-looking and charming and we hit it off straight away. One thing led to another and we spent the night clubbing. He said his aunt had recently arrived in town along with his cousin, and they happened to be staying at the Star. He said his aunt was a great kidder and so was the entire family, and what they loved more than anything was to play practical jokes on one another. So he asked me what room she was staying in, so he could go in and play a joke on her. He said it would be a great laugh, and no one would ever know I was the one who helped him set it up."

"Not only did you give him the room number, but you also provided him with a key, didn't you?" said Boris, still not unkindly, speaking like a favorite uncle.

Susie nodded. "He said he was going to put a rubber spider under his aunt's pillow, and maybe sprinkle some itching powder on his cousin's underpants. He'd tell them later and they would all have a big laugh."

"Only he stole Mrs. Cooper's cat instead, and now he's demanding fifty thousand dollars for the safe return of the animal."

Susie nodded again. "I had no idea he was going to do it, Boris—I swear! When Ben told me just now, I was horrified!"

"He targeted you," said Boris. "He needed access to the Coopers' room and he knew you could supply it."

"I've been used, Boris," Susie sniffed.

"I know," said Boris. "When Ed Cooper told me in confidence about what happened, he suggested an inside job, since the door to his room hadn't been forced, so whoever took his mother's cat must have had a key. So I checked the register, and it didn't take me long to discover that you printed an extra key card, even though Cooper assured me he never asked for one." He leaned back in his chair and sighed. "Susie, Susie, Susie. Now what am I going to do with you?"

"Please, Boris, don't turn me in," the girl begged. "My life will be over and my mom will kill me."

"Your mother is the least of your worries," said Boris, tapping his blotter pensively. "A serious crime was committed, and this episode reflects badly on the hotel—very badly. Already people are talking, and it won't be long before they realize that whoever took that cat must have had help from someone on the inside."

"What am I going to do?" said Susie, sniffling and snuffling and pressing another tissue to her nose. "Oh, what am I going to do!"

"What you're going to do is go to the manager and tell him what happened," said Boris, reaching a swift decision.

"Oh, Boris—but he'll fire me!"

"No, he won't. Not if you're honest and tell him the truth."

Susie didn't seem convinced that the hotel's general manager would show her the same leniency Boris did, but a decision had been made, and it was obvious the head of the reception team was going to stick with it.

"I think you made a serious error of judgment here, Susie," said Boris, "but you're not a criminal, and the only thing anyone can accuse you of is naïveté." He gave her a fatherly smile. "It's all right. Just be more careful next time, will you? And please never print any keys for so-called practical jokers again, even if they are very handsome and charming, mh?"

Susie shook her head ten times in quick succession. "Never again, Boris, I swear. Never again will I do anything like that—ever, ever, ever!"

"I believe you. Now do you want me to go with you?"

"Yes, please," she said in a small voice.

"Well, fine. Let's do that right now. Get it over with." He rose from his chair and so did Susie. Which is when he suddenly caught sight of the feline spies, hiding behind the potted plant. "Oh, for crying out loud!" he said, and in two paces had reached them and grabbed them by the scruff of the neck, one in each hand.

"Ouch!" said Brutus, not all that happy about being caught.

"Put me down, you brute!" said Harriet.

But instead of putting them down, Boris simply marched out of his office, dragging the two of them along with him, and made a beeline for the same kitchen they'd entered the hotel through, kicked open the back door with his foot, and deposited the both of them on the street.

"And stay out!" he demanded, then returned to the kitchen and slammed the door in their faces.

"Clearly that man is a cat hater," Harriet lamented as she checked herself for injuries sustained in the course of their mission. "A brute and a hater of cats!"

"Well, at least now we know what happened," said Brutus, who was actually glad they hadn't suffered a worse fate. He rather liked this Boris fella. He clearly ran a tight ship and was honest to a fault. So what if he didn't like cats lounging about in his office? There are probably worse things a person can get up to. Like seducing innocent and naive young women and taking advantage of them.

Odelia had stepped out of her car and came hurrying up to them. They quickly assured her that all was fine and that they were unharmed, and as they walked back to the car, they related the events as they had transpired.

Odelia was most gratified to hear Susie's story. Most gratified indeed.

Harriet and Brutus, intrepid sleuths, had struck again!

CHAPTER 26

I had placed my ear against the door but frankly I couldn't overhear much of what was going on beyond the door that kept us locked up in that dank room. The faint sound of voices seemed to indicate that wherever we were, it was a pretty large place, with several rooms. Some old house, perhaps, undoubtedly located on the outskirts of Hampton Cove, since we hadn't traveled all that far.

"And so I told Regarda, 'Now look here, raw meat might be all well and good for any other cat out there, but I want my meat cooked, minced and heated to the correct temperature, all right?' I simply cannot digest raw meat, can you?"

"Well..." said Dooley.

"Besides, everyone knows that raw meat is filled with germs and bacteria and all kinds of terrible things. And you don't want me to catch a bug, do you? Or some parasite? Imagine having some terrible worms developing inside my tummy and making me sick! So I told Regarda not to feed me any of that raw stuff ever again, but do you think she listened? Oh, no. Next day she was feeding me the same stuff! And this time fresh from the fridge. Cold raw meat! Imagine!"

"I'm trying to," said Dooley as he threw me uncertain glances.

"But the worst one is Ed. Don't get me started on Ed!"

"You don't have to start on Ed if you don't want to," said Dooley hurriedly.

"Do you know that he once gave me some meat straight from the freezer! From the freezer! I could see the ice crystals attached to the stuff." She shivered. "Yuck! And when I asked him if he was aware that there is such a thing as a microwave, he just gaped at me. No wonder Sara left him standing at the altar. She probably discovered what kind of husband she was marrying." She took a breath, but before we could stop her, continued, "Now don't get me wrong. Ed is the sweetest guy on earth, but you can't feed your cat meat from the freezer. Who does he think I am? A polar bear? A penguin? A *seal*? Ha!"

"Ha ha," said Dooley weakly.

"It wasn't a joke, Dooley," said Aurelie sternly. "I was merely trying to point out to you that even before I was kidnapped and locked up in this horrible place, my life wasn't a bed of roses. Now take last week, for instance. I was doing my business in my litter box when suddenly I realized that it hadn't been cleaned!"

"I hate it when that happens," said Dooley, casting an urgent glance in my direction again. But since I was still trying to pick up some of the conversation our kidnappers were engaged in, I ignored his silent pleas.

"Right?" said Aurelie. "So I told my friend Franny, I said, 'Franny, Regarda has totally forgotten to clean out my litter box again.' You know what she said?"

"Um..."

"She told me to do my business *in front* of the litter box. Not *in* my litter box but *in front*. Teach her a lesson. Make her think. And if that didn't help, the carpet. And as a last resort, the bed. But I'm happy to say she got the message the first time, so I didn't have to resort to the ignominy of having to do my business on the bed. A cat has her pride, after all, and her personal standards. But Regarda never forgot to clean out my litter box ever again. So *that* is how you do it, Dooley. *That* is how you train your humans. It's a tough job but it simply has to be done."

"Good to know," Dooley muttered, sagging a little.

"So have you found a way out of here yet, Max?" Aurelie asked.

"Not yet," I admitted. Though after having been locked up with this talkative cat for going on one hour now I was more motivated than ever to find a way of escape. Not only from our kidnappers but mostly from our fellow prisoner!

"Okay, so you better hurry up," she said. "I need to tinkle and I so don't want to go in that litter box." She made a face. "It's probably the filthiest litter box I've ever had the displeasure of visiting."

"So maybe tinkle on the floor," Dooley suggested. "Teach them a lesson?"

Aurelie gave him a look of distaste. "Some people can't be educated, Dooley. I thought you would know that by now."

"I don't hear Rufus," I said. "I wonder where they took him."

"Out," said Aurelie curtly. "Humans like to take their dogs out."

I could have explained to her that kidnappers are not in the habit of taking their prisoners for a walk, even if they're dogs, but I didn't want her to launch into another monologue. Frankly I found it hard to think in Aurelie's presence. Somehow she took up a lot of space in my head —space I needed to work out a plan of campaign!

I had been pressing my ear to the door again, when suddenly the door yielded to the pressure and I tumbled into the corridor. Johnny had opened the door—possibly to supply us with some much-needed sustenance or to clean out the litter box—and he hadn't counted on the fact that I would be leaning against the door.

I didn't waste any time, though, and skedaddled as fast as my stubby legs could carry me! "Run, Dooley, run!" I cried.

"What about me!" Aurelie said.

I made it as far as the kitchen—or at least a room that looked like a kitchen, located at the end of the corridor. Jerry was seated at the kitchen table, in his shirtsleeves and peeling potatoes for some reason, and another man was also seated there. This one was handsome and somehow reminded me of a movie star—or a photo model. He had one of those sculpted faces with high cheekbones, a square jaw, cleft chin and the clearest blue eyes I've ever seen. His hair was jet-black and neatly quaffed, and the moment I came storming in, he got up, and effortlessly grabbed me by the scruff of the neck and held me up.

"Now what do we have here?" he said with a nasty grin. "Jailbreak? This isn't Chicken Run, little fella. You're not going anywhere."

"Maybe we can let this one go," Jerry suggested. "He belongs to a friend."

"I know who he belongs to," the man said. "And he's staying put and so are his little friends." He turned to Jerry. "Where did you put the big mutt?"

"Out back," said Jerry. "In the kennel."

"Good."

Johnny came storming in, panting a little. He had Dooley dangling from one hand, and Aurelie from the other. "They tried to escape, Gabe," he said. "But I got them just in time."

"Maybe we should tie them up," Gabe said as he studied me with a nasty gleam in his eyes. "Teach them a lesson on how to behave." He shook me a little. "Guests don't run, little fella. Guests stay put and show some gratitude for my hospitality and that of my friends."

He handed me to Jerry, but the latter held up his hands. "Can't you take him? I'm doing the potatoes."

"Why don't you order takeaway like everybody else?" said Gabe.

"I like my French fries fresh," Jerry said. "And so does Johnny. Isn't that right, Johnny?"

"Jerry fries the best fries," said Johnny enthusiastically. "Golden brown and really crunchy on the outside but soft on the inside. They melt on your tongue."

"It's my mother's recipe," said Jerry with a proud smile. "My mother makes the best French fries in the country—possibly the world."

"Fascinating," said Gabe, his voice dripping with sarcasm. "Now are you going to put those cats back or not?"

"Yes, Gabe," said Johnny obediently, and trudged back in the direction he came from.

Just then, Gabe's phone vibrated, and so he put me down, wagging a warning finger in my face and admonishing me to behave, and picked up. "Yes, sir," he spoke into the phone. He listened for a moment, then grinned. "Absolutely, sir. Let's round them all up. Plenty of space here at the farm." He glanced down at me. "No, everything under control. Things are hunky-dory."

And as he spoke, I listened intently to his correspondent's voice, hoping to recognize it. Unfortunately this boss person spoke quietly, and I couldn't make out his part of the conversation. All I knew was that it was a man, and that he was clearly the one in charge, judging from the deferential way Gabe spoke.

"Thanks again for this opportunity, sir," he said now as he raked a hand through his hair. The strands immediately sprang back into place as if by magic. He really had gorgeous hair. "I appreciate it, sir, I really do, and I won't let you down. Yeah, I'll get on that right away. Absolutely. Thank you, sir. Yeah, bye."

He disconnected and Jerry said, "Another assignment?"

"Yep. No rest for the wicked," said Gabe with a wicked grin. "Make sure you're ready to move at midnight."

"Midnight? Where are we going?"

"You'll see," he said, his smile widening.

Jerry's jaw dropped. "The big one?"

"Yep. This is the big one, Jer."

"Oh, goodie!" said Jerry.

Johnny entered on a trot and made a grab for me. At this point I was getting used to being manhandled and allowed him to pick me up. "What's going on?" asked Johnny.

"We're getting ready for the big one," said Jerry, his eyes sparkling.

"Oh, great," said Johnny, but without much excitement. But then he carried me back to my prison cell, so the rest of the conversation eluded me. As he put me down, he gave me a look of apology. "I'm really sorry about this, Max," he said. "If it was up to me I'd let you go. But a job is a job, you know, and Gabe is paying us the big bucks for this."

"You should let us go, you big brute!" Aurelie cried.

"Please don't hold it against me," said Johnny as he patted me roughly on the head. "And I sure hope Marge won't hold it against me either. I like Marge, you know I do. And Odelia, too. But a man's got to make a living. And besides, Jerry thinks it's a good idea, and you know how clever Jerry is. So I figure he's probably right."

"No, he isn't," I said. "He's wrong, and so are you."

"Well, I guess that's just how it is," said Johnny and got up.

"What are you planning to do with us?" asked Dooley.

But Johnny simply gave us a little wave and a goofy smile. "I'll be back to clean out that litter box. And to give you something to eat. But you have to promise to behave this time. No running off on me, you hear? It won't do you any good to run anyway. All the doors are locked."

"Yeah, I thought that might be the case," I said with a sigh.

And then the door closed and the bolt was slammed home.

Now you might wonder why we didn't use the tactic I'd outlined beforehand: clawing and biting and kicking our way to freedom. The thing is that three cats are no match for three humans, unfortunately. We could have caused them some real damage, of course, but at the end of the day, they would have overpowered us, locked us up again, but this time they'd have harbored a serious grudge against us, and you don't want your kidnapper to bear a grudge against you if you can help it, since you don't want him to deposit a big booger in your grub!

"We should have fought them tooth and claw," Aurelie said. "We missed our window of opportunity, you guys. We totally missed it."

"There will be other opportunities," I told her. "We just have to practice patience."

"Easy for you to say," she scoffed. "You don't have to share your litter box with two perfect strangers!"

"Oh, but we're not strangers anymore," said Dooley. "Now that we've been introduced, we're friends, Aurelie."

But Aurelie had other ideas. And as she entered the litter box, she said, "Turn around, you two. And no peeking!"

And so we turned around to allow her to do her business in perfect privacy, her modesty protected by our chivalry.

CHAPTER 27

Fifi felt bad. In fact Fifi felt terrible. If she hadn't deserted her friends in their hour of need, this might never have happened. She would have attached herself to these dastardly kidnappers' ankles and she would have kept snapping until they dropped their evil plan. If only…

Along with the search party, which now comprised the entire neighborhood, she had set out into that field, and had made a beeline for the spot where she had last seen her beloved friends.

Rufus. Max. Dooley…

Oh, why hadn't she stuck around!

The thought of the three of them now being locked up and being subjected to who knows what terrible treatment made her little heart ache. And so she sniffed and sniffed like no tracking dog has ever sniffed before. Police dogs could have taken her correspondence course in sniffing out a trace of the missing person—or pets, as in this case. For Fifi was a dog on a mission. A dog with a purpose. A dog, in other words, who would stop at nothing to find her fellow friends.

It didn't take long for her to pick up the trail, and to follow it all the way to the other side of the field, where the trail ended on the sidewalk, presumably where her friends had been bundled into a marked or unmarked van before being taken away to meet an uncertain fate—a terrible fate—the most terrible fate her fevered imagination could concoct!

But she wasn't deterred. No, sir! Instead she followed that van's trail, and soon a little Yorkie could be seen tripping along the road, sniffing and trying her darnedest to keep up the trail. It wasn't easy, since many cars had passed since that van had gone before. But with bravery bordering on heroism she kept at it—and soon found herself in the suburbs, and glanced up at the house where the van must have parked. And much to her elation, she could definitely smell her good friend Rufus—her dear, dear friend Rufus, whom she had so callously left to his own devices.

The trail led to the house, and when she glanced to the left, she saw movement! A curtain was gently billowing, and behind said curtain, two pairs of keen eyes followed her every movement. She paid them no mind, but went up to the house, and barked ferociously. It didn't take long before those billowing curtains stopped billowing, and the nosy neighborly pair emerged from the house.

As luck would have it, at that exact moment a car arrived, driven by none other than Vesta Muffin, Dooley's human, and pulled up in front of the house. Vesta got out, and so did her friend Scarlett Canyon.

The couple from next door seemed pleased to see the twosome.

"Oh, there you are," said the woman. "I thought you'd never get here."

"I tried to get my son to take an interest," said Vesta, "but he wouldn't budge. Typical."

"Hi, Julia," said Scarlett by way of greeting. "Jack."

"Scarlett," said Jack, looking none too pleased with this new arrival. "You're too late, by the way. The birds have flown the coop."

"And this dog has been barking up a storm," said Julia. "We were just going to see who he might belong to."

"He's a she, actually," said Vesta, "and she belongs to Kurt Mayfield, one of my neighbors." She gave Fifi a keen look. "I'll bet she's looking for the same thing we're looking for: a trace of the kidnappers."

Fifi nodded emphatically. "I am, and if you can help me find them, I'll bite their ankles and then some."

"Okay, Fifi, can you pick up the trail from here? Where did they go, huh?"

Glad that help had finally arrived, Fifi resumed her task of sniffing out the crooks who had snatched her friends, and soon she was barking and pointing with her nose in the direction she thought the van had left.

"She's right, by golly," said Jack, scratching his head. "The van did go that-a-way."

"It did," said Julia. "It turned right at the end of the block."

"Okay, Fifi, do your thing, sweetheart," said Vesta, "and show us what you're made of."

"No way can a dog find the trail of a van," said Jack.

Vesta smiled. "And I'll bet she can. Just you wait and see."

This wholehearted endorsement was music to Fifi's ears, and so she put her nose to the ground again, and was off at a trot, leading the way!

* * *

"SUCH A SAD BUSINESS when people feel so desperate they'll drop off their baby at the nearest hospital," said Emily Doyle. She had checked the baby that had just arrived and shook her head. As a duty nurse at Hampton Cove Hospital she had seen many things in a long career, but she never stopped being touched by the sight of a little baby being dropped off by its desperate mother who couldn't provide for its care due to some personal tragedy.

"She looks well taken care of, though," said her colleague Bonnie. "So whoever her parents are, they nursed her well."

"At least we've got that to be thankful for," said Emily.

The baby, whoever she was, was safely tucked away in her crib, after having received a thorough medical checkup, raising no red flags. By all accounts she was a healthy baby, in excellent fettle.

A little note had been pinned to her bib that read, in a sort of childish crawl, 'Tank U fur tekin caar of dis babie.'

"Clearly this note was written by an illiterate person," said Bonnie as she studied the note once again. "A mother knocked down by the hardships of life."

"Could be a drug addict," Emily suggested.

"Or an alcohol addict," Bonnie imagined.

Emily tucked the baby in with a loving hand and bent over the crib. "We'll take good care of you, little girl. Don't you worry. And we'll find you some new parents who will love you forever."

"I'm sure that whoever left her on our doorstep loved her, too," said Bonnie. "In her own way she probably did what she could."

They smiled down at the little darling, and their heart bled for the person who had been incapable of holding on to this treasure. Then Emily sighed. "Let's call social services. They'll find her a good home with a pair of loving parents."

CHAPTER 28

Night had fallen, and the search of Blake Carrington's field had yielded no result. No baby had been found, which didn't surprise Blake. Now why would a baby crawl into his field and get lost? It wasn't exactly the Amazon rainforest. It might be a sizable piece of land but it wasn't big enough for a baby to get lost in.

Wild theories had been suggested, about Jackie having fallen into a rabbit hole and vanished underground. Or even being snatched by wolves and eaten alive.

As if wolves lived in the heart of this neighborhood. And as if a baby could fall down a rabbit hole and vanish without a trace. Every time a tragedy like this happened, people's imaginations ran wild. He remembered very well from when Steven died and all kinds of crazy theories had done the rounds, some of them even accusing him of being instrumental in his son's death, by sabotaging his car.

And as he walked back to the Pooles' place, he saw that Tex looked thoughtful so he clapped him on the back.

"Don't you worry, Tex. We'll find that baby. It can't have gotten far."

"I'm not worried about that baby," Tex grumbled, as if Blake had said the most outrageous thing. "I'm worried about my gnomes."

"Gnomes? Oh, of course. You're a competitor, aren't you?"

Tex gave him an injured look. "Of course I'm a competitor, Blake. And so are you, and Ted—though it's mainly Ted I'm worried about."

"He's got a nice collection, Ted does," Blake admitted. He was something of a collector himself—as a man who had lost both his wife and his son, the shrink he'd started seeing in the aftermath had suggested he pick up a hobby. It didn't matter what hobby—anything to take his mind off the tragedy that had befallen him. And since he didn't have any particular interest in anything outside the business he'd retired from, the shrink had suggested gnomes. At first he thought the man had gone loco himself, but he was serious, and had given him a primer on the gnome phenom. And so he bought his first gnome at their local garden center. And then a second. And before long, the virus spread, and a sort of rash had taken possession of his sprawling domain, which now resembled a gnome convention, with the little tykes occupying a great part of the available acreage.

"I like gnomes," he admitted. "At first I didn't think I would, but now I'm obsessed with the little fellas."

"I have a portrait of a gnome in my bedroom," Tex said. "My wife hates it, but it's the last thing I look at before I go to sleep at night and the first thing I see when I wake up. I can't explain it, but it sort of soothes me. Gives me peace."

Blake would have mentioned that perhaps the last thing Tex should be looking at before he went to sleep at night was his wife, but he refrained from comment. Far was it from him to judge another man's love life. "Same here," he said instead. "My gnome collection is my proudest achievement. It keeps me sane. Did you know that it was in fact my shrink who suggested I start collecting gnomes?"

"Is that a fact?" said Tex, though it was clear he wasn't really listening, his brow furrowed and his attention elsewhere.

"Oh, yes. All part of my therapy after Steven died."

"Terrible business," Tex murmured absentmindedly. "Terrible."

"It was, and of course I'll never fully recover. But the gnomes help. Anyway, enough about me. So what is bothering you about Ted, Tex?"

Tex looked up from his musings. "Mh? Oh, he's been sabotaging my gnomes. He put chewing gum on Norbert and he chopped off Jackson Brown's nose. He denies it, of course, but I know it was him."

"So what are you going to do about it?" asked Blake, who had always been a man who favored decisive action over idle talk.

"Do? What do you mean, do?"

"If a man destroyed one of my gnomes I'd destroy a dozen of his. An eye for an eye, Tex. It might not be fashionable nowadays, but then I'm not a fashionable man."

"What are you saying, Blake?" asked Tex, his interest piqued.

"I'm saying you need to make it clear to Ted that you won't stand for any of this nonsense." He leaned in. "If I were you I'd take a big ol' hammer, sneak into your neighbor's backyard, and do some serious damage. Really go to town."

Tex snorted, looking shocked. "But-but that's illegal, Blake!"

"I know, but it'll send a message, wouldn't you agree?"

"It would most definitely send a message," said Tex, nodding.

"So what are you waiting for, Tex? What are you, a man or a mouse?"

"Definitely not a mouse," said the doctor thoughtfully. "No, definitely not a mouse."

Blake squeezed his fellow gnome collector's arm. "Just don't get caught would be my advice. It's never a good idea to get caught when doing these things."

And after having delivered this sterling piece of advice, he bid the doctor a good night, and walked back to his car. He glanced up at the sky. Stars had started to twinkle and a full moon had come peeping over the horizon. By all accounts it promised to be a wonderful night.

CHAPTER 29

Harriet, Brutus, Shanille, Kingman, Buster and the rest of cat choir's paying members were intensely worried about the fate that had befallen Max and Dooley—and Rufus, of course, but to a lesser extent. Dogs will be dogs, and probably whatever had happened to Rufus, he only had himself to blame. And so that night cat choir wasn't the scene of gaiety and song but of an urgent meeting to discuss these recent and frankly shocking events.

"We need to find them," Shanille was saying. "It doesn't do for members of Hampton Cove's cat community to be snatched like this. Especially a prominent member like Max."

"And Dooley," Kingman added.

"Yes, and Dooley," said Shanille with a smile.

Whereas Max was one of the pillars of their community, Dooley was such a sweetheart and was beloved by all.

"They'll be sorely missed," said Buster, shaking his head sadly.

"They're not dead, Buster!" said Harriet.

"They might be dead," said Buster. "In fact they probably are. And so is that baby. Fido is convinced they were snatched up by a serial killer. And we all know that serial killers kill—it's what they do."

"Fido is an idiot," said Harriet with decision. "And besides, what does he know? He doesn't know anything," she answered her own question. "Because he's an idiot."

Buster frowned. "My human is not an idiot."

"He is if he thinks that Max and Dooley are dead!"

"Guys, guys," said Kingman, spreading his arms to nip this argument in the bud. "The truth is that nobody knows what happened. Which is what this meeting is all about: to find out where Max and Dooley are, and how to find them and get them back to safety."

"It's not just Max and Dooley," said Brutus. "Aurelie was also kidnapped, and so were Rufus and Jackie Pearce."

"Okay, so who is this Aurelie, exactly?" asked Shanille, who had a hard time following the thread of the story as it was developing.

"Aurelie belongs to a tourist named Regarda Cooper," Brutus explained. "Regarda and her son are staying at the Star Hotel, where a man gained access to their hotel room by sweet-talking a staff member into printing a room key, and grabbed Aurelie. He sent a message demanding fifty thousand dollars for her safe return, and sent a picture as proof of life. This all happened this morning."

"God, what a terrible story," said Buster. "Wait till I tell Fido." He blinked. "Oh, no, I can't tell him—that's too bad."

"Nobody is telling anybody anything," said Shanille. "What we need to focus on right now is to find... What's going on?"

This last question was referring to a sort of ruckus or

fracas that seemed to have broken out on the outskirts of their small gathering. Bright lights had suddenly been turned on, and were pinning them to the spot, blinding them and making it impossible to see what was happening. And then, as near as she could tell, something descended from the sky. It fell on top of her and pressed her down on the ground, as it did the other members of her choir.

The choir leader yelled, "What's happening!"

"The sky! It's falling!" Buster cried.

"I think we've just been caught," said Kingman, who was closest to her.

"Caught? What do you mean, caught!" Harriet demanded.

"It's a net, Harriet," said Kingman. "Someone has thrown a big net on top of us. And if I'm not mistaken, they're going to take us all!"

His words proved prophetic. Since they couldn't move, on account of the big net that had been thrown from above, the members of cat choir were easy pickings. One by one they were being gathered and thrown into the back of a van that had been equipped with steel cages. And before she realized what was happening, strong gloved hands hoisted Shanille up by the neck and carried her over to the van, parked next to one of those bright lights. Without much care for her wellbeing she was shoved into one of the cages, along with Kingman, who unfortunately took up most of the cage real estate, and then the cage door was slammed shut and she was suddenly a prisoner!

"Hey!" she cried. "Let us out of here!"

"I doubt whether they'll be amenable to your suggestion," said Kingman sadly. He settled down on the cage floor. "I just hope they won't demand fifty thousand smackers from Wilbur, cause they won't get it."

"You mean... we've been kidnapped by the same gang

that took Aurelie?" asked Shanille, much perturbed by this development.

"I'm afraid so," said Kingman. He shrugged. "Look at the bright side. At least we'll get to see Max and Dooley again." And after a long pause he added, "And Rufus."

CHAPTER 30

Dan, who had been present at the search party for the missing baby, wondered where his star reporter could have gone off to. Collecting TikTok videos and Facebook stories about the search was all well and good, and he'd already posted a ton of them on the Gazette website, but they were no substitute for an in-depth story from a seasoned reporter. He wanted interviews with all involved, first and foremost the parents of the missing child, and of course Chief Lip, who had personally led the search. Unfortunately Odelia's uncle didn't appear to be big on Facebook, and he wasn't on TikTok either, and neither were the parents.

He'd been trying to reach Odelia, to tell her to write a front-page article about the disappearance of the child, but for some reason she had blocked his calls. He had no idea why, and frankly he was more than a little worried. He would have asked her mom or grandmother, with whom she was close, but they were nowhere to be found, and when he asked Tex, Odelia's dad said he had no idea where his daughter was, nor did he seem overly concerned. For some reason he kept muttering something about gnomes, and wanting to know if Dan intended to devote a special issue to the upcoming Gnome of the Year competition. Since he'd never heard of this elusive competition, he had prevaricated, telling the man he should talk to his daughter, and why not talk to her now?

But Tex had simply made a noise of disgust and had walked away.

So now what? The most shocking event of the week wasn't going to be reported in the Gazette, for even though he had talked to a couple of the people involved himself, he simply didn't have enough material. The parents were too distraught, Chief Lip was too busy, and the participants didn't have anything interesting to say.

So now all he had were TikTok videos, Instagram and Facebook posts and that was it! Not exactly the kind of stuff his paying customers wanted to see on their favorite paper's website. After all, they could easily read all of that social media stuff themselves—and for free!

It was a disaster, that's what it was. And where was Odelia!

* * *

Ed and Regarda were still ensconced in their room, only instead of their old room, they had received an impressive upgrade and were now staying in the Gwyneth Paltrow Suite, one of the best rooms in the house. The general manager of the hotel had personally offered his apologies for the appalling behavior of one of his members of staff, who had been instrumental in the abduction of Regarda's beloved Aurelie, and had expressed the fervent hope that they wouldn't press charges and sue the hotel for substantial damages after this unfortunate incident. Apparently the kidnapper had taken advantage of the naïveté of a young female receptionist and had acquired information and a working key card that had led to the abduction. The young woman had been reprimanded and her imminent dismissal was being considered in connection to this serious error of judgment.

Next, Odelia Kingsley had paid them a visit, this time accompanied by her husband Chase. The two of them had asked their permission to talk to the young woman in question, and have her sit down with a sketch artist so they could start the process of identifying the person who was behind Aurelie's abduction.

Regarda had been hesitant, still mindful of the kidnapper's admonition not to involve the police, but Chase had promised them absolute discretion. And since Ed seemed to think it was a good idea, she had finally relented and given them the go-ahead. In due course a facial composite had been produced and shown to Regarda and Ed, asking whether they recognized the person. Studying the face of the man who had kidnapped her precious Aurelie, Regarda had experienced a wave of an emotion she hadn't understood at first, but later thought must have been justified anger.

"No, I've never seen him before," she admitted.

"Me neither," said Ed, studying the sketch on Odelia's tablet. "So is this the guy who took Aurelie?"

"Yep, that's him," said Odelia. "So now we'll get to work trying to find out who he is, exactly, which will bring us one step closer to bringing Aurelie home to you."

Regarda burst into tears at these hopeful words. "Oh, I hope he hasn't harmed my precious baby." She thought the man looked like a serial killer: all charm and arresting good looks on the surface, but hiding a dark, dark heart underneath.

"It's not just Aurelie who's been taken," said Odelia. "This man has kidnapped our cats, too."

"And a baby and our neighbors' dog," Chase added.

"Oh, God, what is going on!" Regarda cried, much dismayed. She turned to Ed. "Of all the places in the country you could have picked for your honeymoon, you had to pick the one place where a serial kidnapper has decided to go on a rampage!"

"How was I supposed to know that Hampton Cove is the kidnapping capital of the country!" said Ed, not unjustified.

"To be fair, this has never happened before," said Odelia.

"Well…" said Chase, making a face.

"Oh, dear," said Regarda.

"There have been catnappings before," the cop intimated when pressed on the matter. "A local butcher had run out of cheap meat to put in his sausages after his Romanian supplier went bust, so he built an illegal facility where he could produce his own sausages and hired a couple of goons to kidnap cats so he could…" He gave a delicate cough.

"Oh, no!" said Regarda.

"We caught him before… Well, let's just say the factory was shut down."

"Why isn't any of this on TripAdvisor!" Regarda demanded heatedly. "If only I'd known what kind of town this was, I would never have come. Never!"

Just then, Odelia's phone made a dinging sound, and when she checked the message she had just received, her jaw dropped and she paled considerably. She turned to her husband and said, "We have to go, Chase. We have to go now!"

"What is it?" said Regarda. "Have they found Aurelie?

Oh, God. She's dead, isn't she? This horrible man has killed my baby girl!"

"Aurelie hasn't been found," Odelia assured her. "But the kidnapper has just snatched more cats. In fact he has snatched *all* of the cats in Hampton Cove. Every single one of them!"

CHAPTER 31

I don't know what your views are on being kidnapped, but speaking from personal experience I'd say there are three stages: at first you're discombobulated and have no idea what's going on. Then, once you've come to terms with your predicament, you start looking for a way out, and maybe even stage an escape attempt. But at a certain point resignation sets in, and I guess we had reached this stage now, where we had mentally accepted the fact that we were going to be there for just a little while longer. Not indefinitely, as Dooley seemed to think, but it was clear that our imminent release wasn't in the cards.

Lucky for us Aurelie had run out of steam, and had stopped resembling a pandemonium of parrots. Insomuch that I had closed my eyes and was actually on the verge of falling into blissful sleep. I hadn't slept in quite a while, but the events of the past couple of hours hadn't missed their effect and this cat was bone-tired and ready to catch up on some much-needed repose!

Unfortunately it wasn't to be. For just as I was starting

to drift off into the sweet land of dreams, suddenly a loud noise reached my ears.

"What's that, Max?" asked Dooley, who was resting next to me.

"I don't know, Dooley," I said. It sounded like a thousand cats talking at the same time, and at the top of their lungs, too.

"It seems to be coming closer."

"It does. And quite rapidly, too."

"What's going on, you guys?" asked Aurelie, who had woken up from her nap and now stretched herself out on the cold stone floor. "Are they finally coming to rescue us? Is that the United States Marines I hear? Or the FBI? Or possibly a SWAT team?" But then she listened more intently and frowned. "It's cats. And a lot of them. I didn't know SWAT employed cats?"

"They don't. Or at least not to my knowledge," I said. Hope was surging in my bosom. "It must be our friends from cat choir. They must have found us and are here to set us free!"

"Oh, yay!" said Dooley. "Hooray for cat choir!"

"What is cat choir?" asked Aurelie.

"It's our nightly hang-out," I said.

"We sing, we chat, we have fun," Dooley said, summing up the purpose and practice of cat choir to a T. "And we rescue our friends when they're kidnapped!"

"Oh, goodie," said Aurelie, getting up from the floor. "Let's give a warm welcome to our saviors. Three cheers for the heroes!"

The door swung open, but instead of coming face to face with a band of heroic rescuers, we saw a pile of cages, one stacked on top of the other, wheeled in on a hand cart being pushed by Johnny. The big guy took his time unloading the cages, then returned to fetch some more, while his associate Jerry wheeled in a second hand cart, this one also carrying a stack of cages!

I recognized the faces of our friends Kingman, Shanille, Buster, Tom, Tigger, Misty, Shadow, Missy... And Harriet and Brutus!

"Hey, you guys," said Harriet, and she didn't look happy.

"Have you come to rescue us?" asked Dooley eagerly.

"No, Dooley, this is a social call," said Brutus.

"Oh, that's so nice of you!" said Dooley.

"Can't you see we've been kidnapped, you doofus!" said Shanille.

"Kidnapped? What do you mean, kidnapped?"

"They're locked up in cages, Dooley," I pointed out. "So they can't really do a lot of rescuing, now can they?"

"Oh," said Dooley, as if noticing this little detail for the first time. "But that's not good."

"No kidding," Kingman grumbled.

"That's not very nice," Dooley added.

More cages had been rolled in, and by the time the last ones were dispatched, the room was full, with cages stacked high—almost to the ceiling.

"Hey, aren't you going to let us out!" Kingman demanded when Johnny and Jerry made to leave.

"We'll be back to feed you later," Johnny announced, as if he had understood Kingman's words.

"And what if we have to go potty?" asked Harriet, who seemed a little shocked to be locked up like this. "You can't expect us to go potty in these cages!" But apparently this was the big idea, and as Harriet directed first a look down, and her eyes met Shanille's, then a look up, where Brutus was located, she said, "No way!"

"Hold it in, will you, princess?" Shanille said. "You, too, Brutus!"

"Oh, I'll hold it in," Brutus said. After all, if he didn't, both Harriet and Shanille would suffer!

"And I thought *we* had it bad," said Aurelie, stretching out on the floor once again. "Our litter box may not be squeaky clean, but at least I don't have to do my business on top of... well, you know."

"Okay, urgent meeting of cat choir," said Shanille, in spite of her predicament still every inch the community leader. "I don't have to tell you guys that we find ourselves in a bit of a pickle here."

"Tell me something I don't know," a ginger cat pronounced.

"So we have to come up with a plan, people. A plan of escape!"

"We tried to escape," Dooley said. "But they caught us."

"Not what I want to hear, Dooley!" said Shanille.

"It just means your plan wasn't good enough," said Harriet. "Whose plan was it?"

I deferentially inclined my head and earned myself a frown from my cat choir colleagues. "Okay, so maybe it wasn't a good plan, but it was the best one I could come up with," I said in my defense.

"So think, Max!" Brutus suddenly exhorted. "Use that big brain of yours and get us out of this hellhole, buddy! Cause frankly I don't know how long I'll be able to keep this up—or more specifically: in!"

And so I gave myself up to thought. There had to be a way to escape from this place. I closed my eyes and redoubled my efforts. It didn't help that very soon the atmosphere turned into what can only be described as a barroom brawl. Heated arguments broke out over who was to blame for this unwelcome predicament, and there was a lot of yelling and screaming, recriminations flying back and forth.

At one point they got so loud I couldn't hear myself think... until that very noise suddenly gave me an idea. So I gave Shanille a sign, and she used her conductor's voice to summon our friends to pipe down.

And as I explained my big idea, smiles lit up faces left and right and soon my plan was unanimously approved, the consensus being that it was a pippin. And so all eyes turned to Harriet, the latter took a deep breath, smoothed her ruffled fur, and did what she does best.

CHAPTER 32

Fifi had valiantly led the Hampton Cove neighborhood watch through hills and vales and by all accounts should have been exhausted, as Yorkies aren't exactly constructed along the lines of the bloodhound or even the German Shepherd. Still she trudged on, paying no attention to the fact that her paws were starting to complain and that her stomach was rumbling from lack of sustenance. She was going to find her friends and she was going to find them now!

"She's something else, isn't she?" said Scarlett admiringly. "Though maybe I shouldn't have worn my high heels for this excursion."

"I told you to wear your hiking boots," said Vesta.

"I don't have hiking boots."

Vesta rolled her eyes. "Every time," she murmured.

"You know that hiking boots make my ankles look big. I hate them."

And so she traipsed on, taking a break from time to time and making a comment about her feet starting to give her trouble, but otherwise bearing up as bravely as the Yorkie who was leading their select company.

Vesta's phone chimed and she dug it out of the pocket of her tracksuit. "Odelia?" she said as she pressed the device to her ear. She listened with rising indignation and her lips turned into a thin line.

"What is it?" asked Scarlett. "What's wrong?"

But her friend motioned her to silence, then said, "We're still following Fifi to wherever these two bozos took the cats. So if what you're saying is true, this rescue operation has just gotten a whole lot bigger. How many cats were taken, exactly?" Another pause. "All of them? What do you mean, *all* of them?"

Scarlett listened with rising concern. "All the cats were taken? But how? And when? And where? And by who?"

"Whom," Vesta snapped, then spoke into her phone again. "Okay, we'll keep you updated, honey. Don't you worry. Before the night is over, we'll have all of the cats home safe and sound. That's a promise from me to you."

A tall claim, Scarlett thought. They were just a bunch of amateurs, after all, led by another amateur in the form of Fifi. "Okay, so what happened?" she asked when Vesta had tucked her phone away again.

"All the cats were taken."

"What do you mean all?"

"All the cats of Hampton Cove."

"But how is that possible?"

"Cat choir," Vesta snapped.

"Oh, right," said Scarlett, understanding dawning. Ever since she and Vesta had picked up their friendship again, after having been at daggers drawn for years, she had received a crash course in feline life in their fair little town. And one of the things that surprised her was that cats actually have a social life. She always thought they were solitary creatures, hunting solo and avoiding all contact with their ilk. But the cats of Hampton Cove actually gathered every night at the park to join in something called cat choir. They sang their little hearts out and shared the latest gossip and generally fun was had by all.

"Johnny and Jerry would have known about this," said Vesta, looking deeply unhappy. "From close association with Marge, they must have known all about cat choir and decided to make their move."

"But I thought you said they were *simpatico* with Marge?"

"That's what I thought. But this is the last straw. After the stunt they pulled, they're not getting any more sympathy from this family."

They had reached the end of a rutted road that led straight into the woods, and Scarlett started to experience a distinct sense of unease. "I have no idea where we are right now but I don't like it."

"This is the road to old Fraser Bailey's farm," said Vesta. "Has been empty for years. Ever since Fraser died, and his family went to war over the inheritance. The case is in court and will probably be there until the end of time—or until the town council steps in and gets rid of this eyesore."

"I wonder if that's where they took the cats," said Scarlett as she glanced up at some gnarled tree branches that seemed to reach out to them, ready to grab them.

"Wouldn't surprise me one bit," said Vesta, who didn't look happy to be crossing these woods on their own in the middle of the night either.

"Maybe we should call for backup," Scarlett suggested.

"Not until we know for sure we're in the right place. We don't want to make total fools of ourselves again."

As had happened on numerous occasions in the past.

And every time Vesta's son Alec had had to bail them out, which wasn't a lot of fun!

"Okay, so let's ascertain whether the cats are being held at this old farm, and then call Odelia. Agreed?"

"Agreed," said Vesta.

An owl hooted nearby, and they both jumped. "Spooky!" Scarlett whispered.

"Why are you whispering?" Vesta whispered.

"Why are you?"

A branch creaked nearby, and they both shivered.

"Maybe we should call Odelia now!" Scarlett loud-whispered.

But Vesta didn't respond.

"I said—"

"Shush! Listen!"

Scarlett listened. From somewhere in the distance loud caterwauling could be heard, as if a thousand cats were being strangled simultaneously. The sound spurred Vesta into action.

"They're murdering my cats!" she cried, and hurried on.

"Hey, wait for me!" said Scarlett, teetering on her high heels. So against her better judgment she took off her heels and went on barefoot. "Wait up!" she cried, but Vesta was already disappearing around the bend, led by Fifi, who was now barking furiously and running full tilt.

CHAPTER 33

Jerry Vale had never been a big fan of pets of any description. Not that he actively disliked them, but he simply had no use for the creatures and had never understood their appeal. Cats, especially, filled him with disgust. Treacherous creatures, always licking their claws and ready to rip a man to shreds. And so when the assignment landed in their laps to kidnap a bunch of cats, he hadn't exactly been over the moon. But Gabe paid well, and that was all that mattered. Like any small business owner he had to move with the times, and when business was tough in one part of the economy, he had to shift and adapt.

He and Johnny had started their careers as hired muscle and enforcers for a New York real estate tycoon, and when the latter went legit, had become the man's trusted bodyguards. But when their services were no longer required, they had turned to a life of crime once more, with varying success. And so now they were in the business of kidnapping cats and dogs—and babies, but that was an accident. Not unlike a fisherman who accidentally catches a scuba diver in his nets. And just like the fisherman throws the diver back into the ocean, since scuba divers are notoriously hard to digest, they had dumped the baby at the local hospital.

"I don't like this job," he told his long-time associate. "Kidnapping cats and dogs? There must be better ways to make a buck."

"Ooh, but I bet there's big money in petnapping," said Johnny, who was lying on the ratty couch playing a video game. "Just think about those celebrities and their mutts, Jer. I'll bet they pay through the nose to get their yappers back in one piece."

"Yeah, but we're not getting the big money, are we? We're the hired help. In other words: glorified pet sitters. We take all the risks and Gabe gets the dough."

"Gabe took some risk when he kidnapped that first one," said Johnny. "Had to work out some ruse and whatnot. Sophisticated operation, Jer. Real sophisticated."

"If you're saying we're not capable of such an operation you're mistaken, Johnny. We could have snatched that mutt —no sweat."

"I don't know, Jer. He had to seduce some babe. I'm not big on seducing babes, and neither are you. It takes a special set of skills."

"It takes a handsome mug, that's what it takes." Though Johnny was correct in one regard: neither of them possessed that kind of mug. Johnny looked like a gorilla who's been in too many fights and whose face has gotten flattened in the process, and Jerry looked like something that just crawled out of the sewer.

"I think the three of us make a great team," said Johnny, developing his argument. "You're the brains of the outfit, I'm the muscle, and Gabe is the face. Just like the A-Team, you know. Remember that old show from the eighties, Jer?

In that outfit I'd be Mr. T, you're Hannibal and Gabe is Face."

"I'm not the brains," Jerry grumbled. "I don't know what I am, but I'm definitely not the brains. Heck, I don't even know what the plan is." Some guy they never met was calling the shots. Gabe might have seen him, but Jerry and Johnny never had. All they knew was that Gabe called him the boss, and refused to tell them anything more. This mysterious boss was bankrolling the entire operation, and used Gabe as a conduit for his instructions. So far Jerry could make head nor tails of the endgame, if there even was a big endgame. Could be this boss person was making the whole thing up as he went along.

Johnny had picked a big handkerchief from his pocket and something small and pink fell to the floor.

"What's that?" he asked.

Johnny picked it up, then his face cleared. "It's a nose."

"A nose? What are you doing with a nose? Did you kill someone?"

"Not a human nose, silly. It's from one of them gnomes, remember?"

"Oh, right," said Jerry, losing interest.

For some reason Gabe had told them to stake out the Poole place, having developed a particular interest in the doctor. So they'd snuck into the man's backyard, and Johnny had accidentally stepped on one of those stupid gnomes, taking its nose clean off. Then last night they had spent the better part of the night staking out the place. Jerry had gotten so bored he amused himself by sticking a piece of gum all over the ugliest gnome. Lucky for them, Gabe had finally come through with those cameras, so they wouldn't have to go back a third night. But then of course word came from the big boss that the operation was finally a go.

Johnny got up from his couch and stretched. "I better go feed the critters," he said, and disappeared into the kitchen to pick up one of the bags of cat food.

Just then, there was a sort of loud lament, a piercing cry that cut to the bone. Jerry winced as the noise sent shivers running up and down his spine.

"What the heck!" he cried as he jumped up from his chair.

"Must be the cats," said Johnny. "They must be in pain!"

"*I'm* in pain!" said Jerry. "Make them stop, you idiot!"

They both hurried in the direction of the room where they had the cats locked up. And when they opened the door, the noise was deafening, and almost blew them off their feet!

All of the cats, without exception, were screaming as loud as they could, which was pretty loud! And the sound was both shrill and sharp, like nails dragging across a blackboard. It was maddening!

"Make them stop!" he repeated, pressing his hands to his ears. It was to no avail, though, for the screeching seemed to reach deep into his gut and mess around with his insides, twisting them around and tying them into knots.

Johnny approached the nearest cage, and rattled it a little, but it was clear that neither of them was a match for the ferociousness of these terrible beasts. And as if the noise wasn't bad enough, the stench emanating from the room was even worse. One of the cats, or maybe all of them, must have relieved themselves, and the smell was so bad he almost passed out. And as his eyes watered, he could just see how a couple of cats skittered past them and fled down the corridor.

"They're getting away, you fool!" he cried. But Johnny couldn't hear him over all the noise. And when Jerry turned to go in pursuit of the escapees, he tripped and fell over an immovable object. When he looked down, he saw that it was Max, and for a moment his eyes met those of that filthy orange animal. All he could see in Max's eyes was contempt. But before he could make a grab for the fat, hairy beast, Odelia's cat had skipped out and was gone. Oh, crappity crap!

CHAPTER 34

The three of us were going well and moving at a reasonable pace when we arrived in the kitchen. To detect an open window was but the work of a glance, and then we were up on the drainboard, through and away! Landing on all fours, we took a moment to get our bearings, and then we were moving in the direction of town—to find our humans and free our friends. But before we had reached the road, who would we run into but Fifi! And right behind her was none other than Gran!

"Max!" Gran cried, and seemed inordinately pleased to see me. Not as much as I was pleased to see her, though.

Dooley immediately jumped into the old lady's arms and pressed himself to her chest. "I missed you, Gran," he said, burying his head against her bosom.

"And I missed you, Dooley," said Gran warmly.

Panting a little, Scarlett now drew level with us. "Oh, good!" she said. "You found them!"

To my surprise she was barefoot, which didn't seem advisable to me. But we had other things on our mind than

Scarlett's lack of footwear. Our friends were still inside that farm, and might suffer the wrath of Johnny and Jerry once they discovered our escape.

So we relayed our recent adventure to Gran, who took out her phone and called in reinforcements.

"And you must be Aurelie," said Scarlett, crouching down and tickling our new friend behind the ear. "We'll have you reunited with your human in no time, little one."

"I did doo-doo on the floor," Aurelie admitted, looking a little shamefaced. "It was all part of Max's plan. And at first I wasn't in favor, but Shanille convinced me. She's very convincing. And I have to say it worked like a charm. Those crooks were no match for the powerful scent. Though I still think it's in bad taste to do number two on the floor. Number one is fine, and my friend Franny is a big fan of peeing in front of your litter box, or even on the carpet, or the bed, to teach your humans a lesson, as I've explained to Max and Dooley. But I feel like number two is different. Number two is personal. Dogs do it all the time, of course, but then they're dogs, and one expects such behavior from a dog. But cats are different. We have higher standards. As I told my best friend Franny that time, 'Franny,' I said, 'there is a time and a place for number two and this is neither the time nor the place.' We were in church at the time, waiting for Ed's fiancée to show up so they could get married. She never did show up, but of course we didn't know that."

"You're quite the talker, aren't you?" said Scarlett with a smile.

"You have no idea," I said with a deep sigh.

"They're sending in the troops," said Gran with a look of satisfaction.

"What troops?" asked Dooley. "Are they sending in the army?"

"My son's troops," Gran clarified. She turned to me. "Was the baby in there with you?"

"No, they said they were dropping her off at the hospital," I said. "Apparently they had no use for a baby."

"Where is Rufus?" asked Fifi anxiously. "Is he in there?"

"No, he's out back," I said. "Locked up in a kennel."

"Oh, no, not a kennel!" said Fifi. "Rufus hates kennels." And before we could stop her, she was tripping away in the direction of the old farmhouse.

"See?" said Gran triumphantly. "I told you they were keeping them at the old Bailey farm."

"Poor babies," said Scarlett as she surveyed the farm, which even in the moonlight looked dilapidated and long past its prime. "They kept you in there, did they? Probably fed you water and stale bread?"

"No, they fed us kibble," I said. "But not the good kind."

"A cheap brand," Aurelie specified. "Absolutely yucky."

And as we watched on, suddenly two figures appeared. They were Johnny and Jerry, and they were hurrying in the direction of their van.

"They're getting away!" said Gran. "We have to stop them!"

"Don't you worry about a thing," said Scarlett, and rummaged around in her purse for a moment, before unearthing two cans of pepper spray. She held one out to Gran, the two ladies exchanged a smile, and Gran took the offered can.

"Let's do this," said Gran, and they both headed for the van.

There was the sound of an engine being induced to play ball, coughing and sputtering but refusing to tick over. The grinding sound was interspersed by loud cursing, but before Jerry had any luck with his van, the two members of the neighborhood watch had reached them, and judging from the screams, the tools of their particular trade met their mark. It was game over for the criminal duo.

* * *

RUFUS HAD to admit that he'd seen better times. Not only did he thoroughly dislike being cooped up inside a kennel, but the food these people had picked out for him was decidedly below par. Not only was it probably past its sell-by date, but it tasted like cardboard. More than the food and the accommodation, though, he missed his friends. Especially Fifi. He liked Fifi, and had from the first. She was such fun to be around. A sunny personality who never failed to cheer him up. He himself had a tendency to gripe and grumble and grouch when things weren't going his way, but never Fifi. She was sociable and liked by all.

He had placed his large head on his paws and had closed his eyes, resigning himself to his fate. And as he lay there, he could just imagine Fifi's voice as she called out to him. 'Rufus,' she said. 'Rufus, where are you?' 'Over here,' he would say. 'Over here, Fifi.'

He smiled and thought this was such a nice dream. But then Fifi's voice seemed to grow even louder and he frowned and opened his eyes. Almost as if she was right there. Which was impossible, of course.

"Rufus!" suddenly her voice rang out. "Rufus, where are you!"

But… how was that possible? He sat up immediately. "Over here, Fifi!" he cried. "I'm right over here!"

And suddenly there she was: Fifi, his best friend, rounding the corner and heaving into view!

She halted in her tracks for a moment, as if she couldn't believe her eyes. But then she skipped right up to him, looking as joyful and happy as ever. "Rufus!" she cried as she hopped and jumped and generally behaved like a gamboling puppy. "Oh, there you are!"

"And there *you* are!" he cried, sniffing her nose and giving it a lick through the chicken wire. Oh joy, oh happy day!

"We have to get you out of this horrible thing," said Fifi.

"I've tried," he said, "but they've got it locked down tight."

"Don't you worry, Rufus," said Fifi. "Vesta is here, and her friend Scarlett, and pretty soon the entire Hampton Cove police force will also be here."

"And Ted and Marcie?" he said hopefully.

Fifi laughed. "I'm sure they'll be here, too."

"Oh, good," he said. Though secretly he was mostly glad that Fifi was there. But he didn't tell her, of course. Fifi was his best friend in all the world, and he was too clever to ruin such a beautiful friendship by uttering sentimental slop!

But then Fifi suddenly looked coy. "Rufus?"

"Fifi?"

"I've missed you."

"And I've missed you."

"I was afraid you were… you know."

"I know," he said. "But I'm fine."

"I'm glad. Boy oh boy, am I glad." For a moment they didn't speak, only listened to the cats caterwauling, then Fifi said, "Rufus?"

"Fifi?"

"I missed you."

"And I missed you."

"No, but I *really* missed you," she said, and gave him a meaningful look.

He grinned. "And I *really* missed you, too."

And when they rubbed their noses together this time, it was with just a little more fervor than before. It was the beginning of a beautiful affair.

CHAPTER 35

It didn't take long for Uncle Alec and his officers to arrive on the scene and for our kidnappers to be arrested and carted off. Soon the old farm was the scene of a happy reunion, with pet parents driving up from far and wide to be reunited with their beloved pets. Marcie Trapper was there, of course, to pick up Rufus, but also Regarda and Ed Cooper, Wilbur Vickery (Kingman's human), Fido Siniawski (Buster's human), Father Reilly (Shanille's human) and so on and so forth.

The list is long, and it would carry me too far to rattle it off in full. Suffice to say that the place turned into a beehive of activity and that tears of joy were plentiful and shed without shame or inhibition. And I have to say that when I was reunited with Odelia, I also got a little emotional. Even Brutus's eyes were moist when Chase clasped him in his arms, and Harriet blubbered uncontrollably when Marge arrived. And when word reached us that Jackie had been found safe at our local hospital, and had been reunited with her distraught parents, it added to the general atmosphere of relief and the notion that finally all was well with the world again.

"Okay, so we've got Johnny and Jerry," said Chase, who stood discussing the state of affairs with his superior officer. "But where is the guy who snatched Aurelie from her hotel room?"

"Beats me," said Uncle Alec, scratching his thinning mane. "According to Johnny his name is Gabe, and he wasn't working alone but answered to someone he referred to as the boss."

"Gabe, Gabe..." said Chase as he checked his phone. "This wouldn't be Gabriel Martinez, by any chance, would it?" He glanced over to the Coopers, who stood lavishing their attention on Aurelie, and walked over for a moment. He held out his phone. "Could this be the man who took Aurelie?" he asked, and deliberately held the phone so that Aurelie could see the picture.

The Coopers shrugged. "We never saw him, detective," said Regarda.

"You should ask this receptionist person," said Ed.

But Aurelie had studied the picture closely and now nodded. "Yep, that's him," she said. "That's the uncouth miscreant who manhandled me and refused to clean out my litter box! I hope you catch him and teach him a lesson, sir!"

And so I nodded to Chase, who gave me a wink. Walking back to Uncle Alec, he whispered, "We make a good team, don't we, Max?"

"We sure do," I confirmed. Now if he would just learn our language already!

"Okay, so it's him," said Chase as he joined Uncle Alec.

"I'll send out an APB," said Uncle Alec, and grabbed for his phone.

Suddenly a loud yell came from the farmhouse, and

when we looked up, we saw that one of Uncle Alec's officers was waving us over. He was standing next to an old water well. Part of the well had collapsed, but judging from the way the officer stood looking down, it wasn't blocked.

"There's a body down there," the officer announced, and shone a flashlight so his boss could verify this statement.

Uncle Alec took a glance at the spot indicated and winced. "Looks like our friend Gabe didn't make it."

"It's him?" asked Chase as he bent over to take a peek. "Ouch," he said once he had. "Is that..." He narrowed his eyes. "Can you shine that light over there, buddy?" Once the officer had, he pointed down. "See?"

"Oh, yeah, I see it now," Uncle Alec confirmed.

"What is it?" asked Odelia, who had joined us.

"He's got a neat little hole in his forehead," said Uncle Alec. "And if I'm not mistaken, that just might be a bullet hole."

"So he was murdered?"

"That would be my conclusion." He stepped back from the abyss. "I better call Abe," he said, referring to the county coroner. "Looks like we've got a murder on our hands, people."

"Falling out among thieves?" Chase suggested.

Uncle Alec nodded, but then the call connected and he walked away to apprise Abe Cornwall of recent events.

"You don't think Johnny and Jerry did this, do you?" asked Odelia. "They're thieves and kidnappers, but not murderers, surely?"

Chase shrugged. "Too soon to tell, babe, but I don't see anyone else around, do you?"

And so all of a sudden our kidnapping case had turned into a murder case. And just when I was looking forward to finally enjoying that long-desired nap!

Harriet and Brutus came sidling up to us. "That was a pretty solid idea you had in there, Max," said Brutus. "To sing our way to freedom."

"Well, it seemed only logical when the entire cat choir was locked up to use our secret weapon to create a distraction," I said, referring to Harriet's powerful soprano voice.

"I hope I didn't overdo it," said Harriet modestly. "I have to say I found the experience exhilarating. Like a performance at the Metropolitan Opera, you know, or Madison Square Garden."

"You definitely generated the same amplification," I said. Though confined to such a small space, her voice had probably cracked the paint on the walls. It certainly served to cause some serious pressure on the eardrums of all those present, first and foremost our abductors, which was the whole idea, after all.

"Why are Chase and Odelia looking down that well?" asked Brutus.

"There's a body down there," Dooley announced. "He's been murdered!"

"Murdered!" Harriet said, taken aback by this piece of news. "But who is he?"

"Gabriel Martinez," I said. "He's the man who organized these kidnappings, and Chase thinks Johnny and Jerry might be behind the murder."

"I knew they were bad," said Harriet with a look of distaste. "But I didn't know they were this bad!"

"It may have been someone else," I said, but Harriet wasn't having any of that.

"Oh, no. If Chase says it was them, it must be them. He's the detective, and I trust his judgment. And also," she added on a slightly simpering note, "he saved us from this ordeal. He's such a hero."

I could have told her that it was actually Fifi who saved

the day, but she was already sashaying over to Chase, to rub against his leg.

"Looks like it's case closed, eh, Max?" said Brutus. "What a day," he added, shaking his head. "What a day!"

"You can say that again," I agreed, and yawned. When I had finished, I saw that he was regarding me sharply. "What?"

"So about that Master Soporific Word," he began.

"Oh, not now, Brutus!" I said. "I just went through this great ordeal!"

"We all went through this great ordeal, Max. And now I would like to get some sleep. So how about it? Have you finally remembered?"

"I don't know if you've noticed, but I've been a little busy today."

"You were locked up in there for hours, Max!" he cried. "You had plenty of time to remember. So what is it? What's the magic word?"

"Lollygag, all right!" I said, spitting out the first word that came to mind.

He blinked. "Lollygag?"

"That's right. Lollygag."

"So if I keep repeating that word I'll fall asleep?"

"Absolutely. You have my personal guarantee."

"A personal guarantee from Max means something," he said, and gave me a grateful nod. "Why, thanks, buddy. I'm going to try it straight away." He clapped me on the shoulder. "I knew you'd come through. Harriet figured this soporific word stuff was probably a load of nonsense, but I told her that if Max says this word exists, it exists." And with these words, he walked off in the direction of Odelia's car, presumably to curl up on the backseat and lollygag himself to sleep.

I gulped a little, then told Dooley, "Maybe it's time to go home."

"Great. Let's hop into Odelia's car so she can drive us."

"Let's walk," I suggested. "I feel like walking."

"But why walk if Odelia can drive us?"

"It's a beautiful night," I said, gesturing to the sky. "The moon… the stars… And besides, walking is good for you. Slimming, and inducive to good health."

"But…"

"Dooley, if Brutus finds out that my so-called soporific word doesn't work, he won't be too well pleased. And frankly I don't want to be around when he does find out, do you?"

Dooley's eyes went a little wider, then he started walking at a rapid pace.

"Not that way!" I called after him. "This way!"

"Gotcha!" he said, and so together we set out to put as much distance between ourselves and Brutus as felinely possible!

CHAPTER 36

Night had fallen, darkness had descended on the backyard of Ted and Marcie Trapper and not a soul stirred. Or did it? For suddenly the soft sound of a footfall could be heard, disturbing the quiet of the night. An intruder had entered the backyard, and stood regarding the Trappers' domain, a look of determination on his face. In his hands, the intruder clasped a sledgehammer, and as he approached Robert Parker, Ted Trapper's prize gnome and the pride of his collection, the hammer was heaved high, and for a moment hung suspended in the air.

All nature held its breath, and the next moment the hammer came down with a loud crash on the gnome's head, reducing the plaster creature to a pile of dusty fragments of what once had been a proud gnome.

Oddly enough, the moment the hammer struck, there was an echo. The intruder looked up from his vile work and listened attentively. But when nothing more could be heard, he figured it must have been the work of his imagination.

He eyed his destructive work with a smile of satisfaction, then hoisted the sledgehammer from the rubble and returned whence he came. And as he made his way across the hedge, it was almost as if he could sense a presence nearby. So he halted, and waited, and listened again. But when nothing stirred, he carried on, and soon was in bed, wondering where his wife could have gone off to.

THE NEXT MORNING, bright and early, Tex opened his eyes and blinked against the light streaming in from the window. Marge was back and lying right next to him. She stirred, and he kissed the top of her head.

"Gorgeous day," he announced happily. It was the day of the Gnome of the Year contest, and he had an idea he just might be a real contender. At any rate, he knew who wasn't a contender: his next-door neighbor Ted!

"You're looking happy this morning," said Marge as she rubbed the sleep from her eyes.

"You weren't in bed last night when I went to sleep," he said. "Up late?"

"I got a call from Odelia. They found the cats."

"They found the cats! Oh, but that's great, honey!"

He had been vaguely aware that some cats had gone missing, but frankly he'd had so much on his mind that he hadn't paid a lot of attention. But if Marge was happy, he was happy. Oh, this day was getting better every minute!

"I was looking for you," said Marge, sitting up. "Where were you?"

"Out," he said curtly. "At Costco. I needed some gardening tools."

"Oh, that's right. Your big contest. That's today, right?"

He smiled a bright smile. "Indeed it is, treasure of my being. And I won't conceal from you the fact that I just might be a real contender."

"Of course you are. I keep telling you, Tex, you just have to keep the faith."

He laughed a careless little laugh.

"What?" she asked.

"Oh, nothing. Just that a person needs a little more than faith to win in a big competition like this. One needs a plan!"

"What plan?" she asked, a frown suddenly marring her brow. When he didn't respond, she said, "Tex, what did you do?"

"Nothing. Just tipping the odds in my favor a smidgen."

"Tex, now you're scaring me—what did you do?"

"Something I should have done a long time ago."

"You didn't do anything foolish, did you?"

"I did something very smart—and heroic. After all, when someone strikes at the heart of your domain, you have to strike back and—Aargh!"

He had hopped from the bed and had moved over to the window. The moment he threw the curtains wide, the first thing he saw was Norbert—or at least what was left of Norbert: nothing but a pile of dust!

"Honey!" Marge cried, and quickly joined him at the window.

"N-N-N-Norbert!" Tex stuttered, shocked to the core.

"Where is he?" asked Marge.

"He's gone! Destroyed!" Instantly his mood went from jubilant to shocked to enraged. "Ted! He did this! But I'll show him!"

"Looks like someone already did," said Marge, and pointed to where Ted's prime gnome Robert Parker had stood. Now all that remained was a little collection of dust and colorful shards. She patted her husband on the back. "A gnome for a gnome. Are you sure you and Ted aren't secretly identical twins?"

And with a smile she put on her dressing gown and trotted down the stairs.

So that was the echo he heard last night. At the exact same time he was destroying Robert Parker, Ted was taking a whack at poor Norbert!

And as he was staring from Robert Parker to Norbert and back again, his neighbor appeared, sadly glanced down at the remnants of his precious gnome, then up at Tex, his face working furiously.

Their eyes met, and Tex saw that Ted knew, just as he knew.

Suddenly the doorbell rang, and he jerked his head up.

It was the jury. They were early. Not that it mattered. Without Norbert to lead the pack he didn't stand a chance. There was one consolation, though: without Robert Parker, Ted didn't stand a chance either.

In other words: mutual assured destruction.

CHAPTER 37

Jerry wasn't happy, and neither was Johnny, though the latter had a way of looking at things that bordered on the philosophical. The two crooks were locked up in the slammer, and had just been through a grueling two-hour interrogation.

"I'm sure it'll all work out," the big guy said as he intertwined his fingers on his big belly and relaxed. He liked prison. It was like a second home to him.

"Work out?!" Jerry cried. "What are you talking about? We're in prison, Johnny! In prison! And now they're trying to pin a murder on us!"

"Oh, I'm sure that's just a big coincidence," said Johnny, which was exactly what he had told that nice Chase Kingsley, Marge's son-in-law.

"A coincidence! The guy is dead! Murdered!"

"I don't think so," said Johnny. "He probably fell and hit his head."

"He has a bullet hole in his head, Johnny!"

"I'm sure he doesn't. Probably a smudge."

"They dug a bullet out of his skull!"

"Must be a mistake. Even cops make mistakes, you know." He gave his friend and associate a reassuring smile. "Just you wait and see. They'll figure out that we got nothing to do with Gabe falling down that well and they'll let us walk free."

Jerry stared at him as if he'd lost his mind. "I'm starting to think that *you* fell down that well and hit your head," he said nastily.

"Wake me up when breakfast gets here, will you, Jer?" said Johnny, closing his eyes. "I didn't sleep a wink last night." And soon the only sounds that could be heard were soft snoring from one corner, and the grinding of teeth from the other.

* * *

A MEETING HAD BEEN ARRANGED and was taking place in Uncle Alec's office, and Dooley and myself had been invited. Or I should probably say that Odelia had inserted us into the office without invitation. Uncle Alec had given us a dirty look but hadn't said anything. He was probably too tired to bother. Also: we were the recent victims of the heinous crime of kidnapping, so a little leniency on the 'No Pets Allowed!' policy was appreciated.

Chase was also there, and he gave those present a quick overview of the results of his interviews with Jerry Vale and Johnny Carew.

"They admit to everything except the murder," was the gist of Chase's report. "They admit to the kidnappings, working for Martinez, the intention to make bank on the ransom, etcetera etcetera."

"But not to the murder of their associate," said Uncle Alec.

"But why?" asked Odelia. "Why admit to one thing and

not the other?"

"Because murder carries a bigger penalty than kidnapping," said Chase. "Too bad the cats weren't there when it happened. They might have been able to provide some clue. Some evidence."

"Okay, so it's still early days," said Uncle Alec. "I'm sure the forensic team will come up with something. Vale and Carew aren't exactly criminal masterminds. If they killed Martinez, and I don't think there's any doubt that they did, they must have left some traces. Blood on their clothes or shoes, their DNA on Martinez." He placed his hands on his desk. "A confession would have been easier, but if they want to do this the hard way, then that's what they get. One way or another, we'll get them for this. So how far are we on identifying Martinez's contact? The one feeding him instructions?"

"Nothing yet," said Chase. "We checked his phone but it looks as if whoever was behind this whole thing used a burner phone. Untraceable, I'm afraid. And Vale and Carew claim they didn't know who Martinez was working for either." He leaned forward. "They did provide one piece of startling new information."

We all looked up at this, and Uncle Alec placed his beefy forearms on his desk. "What?"

"According to them, whoever was in charge of the operation wanted them to destroy all the pets they caught."

"Destroy them!" Odelia cried.

Chase nodded grimly. "First they were going to extort as much ransom money from the owners as they could, but ultimately they were never going to release them. The plan was to destroy every last one of the pets and dump them in front of Town Hall. Which is when Vale and Carew got into a serious argument with Martinez, since they hadn't signed up for such carnage and didn't agree at all."

"This could be the moment they got into that fight and fatally shot Martinez," said Uncle Alec, nodding. He seemed pleased. "Progress, people. We're definitely making progress here. Good work, Chase. Keep it up." He glanced down at Dooley and me. "So how are the cats? Any, um, trauma?"

"They seem to be fine," said Odelia. "They slept all night, and this morning when I woke up they were still asleep, which is understandable, after everything they went through. But they ate well, and they seem okay to me. Even Dooley."

Dooley frowned. "What does she mean by that, Max? 'Even Dooley?' Why 'even Dooley?'"

"I think she thinks you're the more sensitive of her four cats," I said. "And so possibly the one most affected by this kidnapping."

"Oh," said Dooley, and thought about this for a moment. "So… is that a good thing or a bad thing, to be 'sensitive?'"

"It's not necessarily good or bad, it's just the way you are, Dooley. And that's fine."

"Okay," he said, looking much relieved. "I was starting to think there might be something wrong with me."

"There's nothing wrong with you, buddy," I said. "Nothing at all."

"So do you think Johnny and Jerry did this?" he asked.

"I'm not sure. It's possible, of course. Maybe they fell out over this crazy plan to murder all the pets, or over the ransom money, over how they were going to divide it. It could have been anything, really. This Gabe person was a tough cookie, and Jerry is no pussycat either."

Dooley laughed. "I know, Max. He's a human, not a cat!"

I smiled. "I meant that if Gabe and Jerry went toe to toe,

Jerry would have given as good as he got. Though from what Chase told us just now it seems that the gun that was found at the bottom of the well didn't have any fingerprints. Jerry could have wiped them, of course."

There was still something about this case that was nagging me, though I couldn't put my finger on what it was, exactly. Odelia, who likes to be thorough when it comes to these cases, had made a list of possible suspects who could have killed Gabe, in the unlikely case Johnny and Jerry were innocent, as they claimed.

Apparently Gabe's wife had recently announced she wanted to be his ex-wife instead, after catching her husband in the act with the neighbor's wife in their marital bed—Gabe's bed, not the neighbor. And consequently the neighbor wasn't happy with Gabe either. So those two had a solid motive to get rid of him.

And then there was Gabe's former boss. Franklin Beaver owned a hardware store in town, and Gabe had worked for him after he graduated from college. Franklin had nothing but good things to say about Gabe, except for the fact that he had caught him with his wife one morning, in his office—Franklin's office, not Gabe's. Franklin had fired Gabe on the spot, and divorced his wife. So she was upset with Gabe, too. This all happened a couple of years ago, though, so I didn't see why either of them would suddenly decide to go and murder the man now.

Still, it brought the list of potential suspects up to four. Six when you included Johnny and Jerry.

Odelia and Chase were going to interview all of these people today, even though Uncle Alec assured them this was a waste of time, since they already had Gabe's killers in custody. But our humans were going ahead anyway.

I would have accompanied them, and so would Dooley, but we were still a little low on sleep, and so we decided to return home and catch up on some much-needed slumber instead.

Odelia dropped us off at home, and when we entered the kitchen through the pet flap, we found that Harriet and Brutus had selected our favorite couch to put in some more nap time, too. When we walked in, Brutus beamed at us. "Amazing stuff, Max, this word of yours. I haven't slept so well in years!"

"Lollygag," said Harriet, rolling the word around her tongue. "I have to admit I was wrong, Max, and you were right. It's wonderful to be able to sleep so well. Or should I say to lollygag, ha ha!"

"Ha ha," I said a little weakly.

"Ha ha!" said Brutus heartily. "Come here, Maxie baby —our savior!" And to show his affection he grabbed me by the head and gave me a noogie. "Isn't he just the greatest?" he said as I rubbed the injured spot.

"You didn't let us down, Max," said Harriet. "You came through, and for that I want to salute you with a song." And so she gave me an awkward sort of salute by bringing her paw to her temple. "This is for you, sir," she said, and opened her mouth to launch into song. And before we could stop her, we were treated to her rendition of Ariana Grande's *One Last Time*. But when she sang, 'I need to be the one who takes you home,' Brutus loudly cleared his throat and started clapping.

"Great song, cuppy cake! Wonderful! And now let's all settle down and do some more 'lollygagging!'"

And so we did as he suggested, and distributed ourselves across different sections of the couch. Before long only the sound of soft snoring could be heard—except from me, for I'd just had an idea, and no amount of lollygagging could keep me from exploring it to its inevitable conclusion.

CHAPTER 38

Frankly Ed didn't feel like sticking around any longer. If he'd had his reservations about going on this honeymoon with his mom before, he now felt it had been one big mistake. If they hadn't come, Aurelie would never have been taken, and his mom and her cat would have been spared the aggravation the past twenty-four hours had brought. But when he told his mother that it was probably time to go home, she protested loudly.

"Are you kidding? Just when they're suggesting to pay for another two weeks? In their best suite? All expenses paid? You can go home if you want, but I'm staying put, and so is Aurelie. Isn't that right, sweetness?" She cuddled the apple of her eye, and even though Aurelie made a sound of protestation, at least she didn't seem to have suffered any permanent damage from her ordeal.

"I don't know, Mom," said Ed as he looked out across the rooftops of the houses in the direction of the ocean. The suite had the best view, the manager had assured them, and he hadn't been kidding. "I mean, hasn't this kidnapping business spoiled things for you? It has for me. I don't feel like lying on the beach after what happened. I don't think I'll be able to relax, you know. And besides, how can you relax on the beach and leave Aurelie in the room alone?"

"Oh, but I'm not leaving her alone in the room," said Regarda.

He frowned. "What do you mean?" He noticed his mom had a sort of mischievous look in her eyes, and he wasn't sure he liked it.

"I've hired a cat-sitter!" she said.

He made a face. "Are you sure you can trust this person? You never know if they might not be connected to this same gang."

"Oh, I'm absolutely sure she's not connected to this gang."

"So how do you know that this woman will get along with Aurelie? I don't have anything against your cat, but you have to admit that Aurelie is very particular about who she likes or doesn't like." Aurelie had once scratched one of her cat-sitters back home when he didn't feed her quickly enough to her liking. She might look like a sweetheart, but Mom's cat had quite the temper.

"Oh, I know for a fact that she will get along with Aurelie just fine. And that's because they already met—several times."

"Several times? You mean it's someone you know?"

"And someone you know, too," said Mom, and her eyes were twinkling. Ed eyed her suspiciously. Now what was she up to?

A knock sounded at the door, and he shouted, "Yes, come in!" As he looked up, he saw a familiar person stride into the room. It was Sara, his absentee bride-to-be! He got up from his chair so quickly it toppled over. "Sara!" he cried. "What-what-what are you doing here?"

"She's my new cat-sitter," Mom announced. And to show Ed she wasn't kidding, Aurelie pranced up to Sara and stroked her leg. "See? She's perfect!"

"But-but-but..." he stuttered, this sudden meeting leaving him speechless.

"I know the last person you expected to see was me," said Sara, who looked as radiant and lovely and beautiful as ever. In fact even more so, Ed thought. "And I have to admit that when Regarda called and suggested I fly down here I had my reservations. But then we got to talking, and pretty soon I realized I've made the biggest mistake of my life."

"What do you mean?" asked Ed, finding his tongue again.

Sara took a step closer and Ed took a step back.

"The reason I wasn't at the wedding is because the night before someone sent me a series of pictures of you in the arms of another woman," she said. "Kissing, too. The time stamp told me they were taken a week before the wedding. The person who sent them also claimed the girl was pregnant."

He blinked a couple of times. "Pregnant? Pictures? I-I don't understand. What woman? What are you talking about?"

"It was Jessica, Ed. They sent me pictures of you and Jessica."

He blinked some more, prey to complete confusion. Jessica was a girl he'd gone to college with. They'd gone out a couple of times, but then Ed had met Sara and that was it. He knew she was the one for him, and so he had gently broken the news to Jess and told her she was one of his dearest friends, but nothing more, and even though she was a little disappointed, she had accepted that's how it was.

And now this.

"But I never… I mean we were never… that never happened. I haven't seen Jess in months. Who-who sent these pictures?"

"Well, I never questioned that they were real, given the fact that you and Jess were an item before we met, but like I said, I got to talking to Regarda, and I told her what happened, and she said it couldn't possibly have been you in those pictures, because you were in Whaleyville helping your uncle when they were supposedly taken."

"The timestamp," Mom explained. "It was the weekend you helped George drive that load of firewood to his place."

"But…" said Ed, still not fully understanding.

"I called Jessica," said Regarda. "After my conversation with Sara I called your ex-girlfriend and asked her straight out if she doctored those pictures and sent them to Sara to sabotage your wedding. After a lot of hemming and hawing she broke down and admitted the whole thing. Said she was still in love with you, and she hoped to get you back once Sara was out of the way."

"What?!"

"It's true," Mom assured him. "She was going to be there for you—a friend to fall back on. And then she'd win you back. Only this honeymoon sort of messed up her plans."

"I don't believe this," said Ed, raking a hand through his hair. "And you believed this? Just like that?"

"The pictures were very convincing, Ed," said Sara.

"They were," Mom confirmed. "I would have believed them."

"Look, I know I probably should have called you and confronted you," said Sara. "And that's on me and for that I apologize." She looked rueful. "But it hasn't been easy, Ed. It's not a lot of fun to get photographic evidence of your fiancé with another woman on the eve of what should have been the happiest day of your life."

"No, I can see that," he admitted. "What Jess did is terrible, and I still find it hard to believe that she would do such a thing, but..."

"Oh, don't be like that, Ed," said Mom.

"Like what?"

"Just kiss and make up already!"

Both Ed and Sara turned to Mom. "What?!" they both cried at the same time.

"You two love each other, everyone can see that, and just because some psycho ex-girlfriend ruined your wedding doesn't mean you should let her ruin the rest of your life as well. So I'm going to leave this room, and when I get back in half an hour I want to see nothing but happy faces."

"But, Mom!"

"No buts, young man! I almost lost my precious Aurelie, so you owe me some good news, all right?" And with these words she walked to the door.

"Mom!" said Ed.

"Happy faces!" she admonished them, and walked out.

Ed stood staring at the closed door for a moment. "Can you believe her?"

"I can," said Sara with a grin. "So what about it, Ed? Are you going to forgive me or what?"

"I'm not sure," said Ed, and he wasn't.

"After all, I forgave you."

"For something I didn't do!"

"You could have done it. I still have the evidence on my phone."

"Oh, please," he said, and crossed his arms in front of his chest, the picture of the implacable male whose ego has been badly hurt. "I stood there in front of both our families, all of our friends... looking like a complete moron!"

"Oh, that's right. I saw the video Danny shot. That was pretty hilarious. Though I have to admit at the time I felt you deserved it, after what you did to me."

"I didn't do anything!"

"I know, I know," she said. He noticed how she had somehow closed the distance between them, even though he hadn't seen her move. She placed a hand on his arm. "Is that a smile I see?" she teased. "A teeny, tiny smile?"

"No, it is not," he insisted.

"Oh, don't be like that," she said.

He rolled his eyes. "Why does everyone keep saying that?"

"I came to our honeymoon, didn't I? We might not technically be married but here we are, in our honeymoon suite." She glanced around. "I don't remember booking this suite, though. This must be costing you a fortune."

"We got an upgrade," he said. "After Aurelie was kidnapped, they discovered the kidnapper had an accomplice who works for the hotel, so the manager apologized and gave us this suite. He hopes we won't sue."

"How is Aurelie?" she asked, as she regarded the cat keenly.

Aurelie sat grooming herself in a sunny spot on the floor and looked absolutely fine, as if nothing had happened. "Cats are resilient," he said. And so, he thought, was he. And as he studied Sara, who had now crouched down next to Aurelie and was stroking the cat gently, he realized he did still love her, and that he had already forgiven her for whatever happened with those pictures of Jess.

"It's going to be crowded in here," he said finally.

She looked up, her golden tresses shifting. "What do you mean?"

"You, me, my mom. It's going to be crowded in this suite."

"It'll be fine," she said, as she removed a tiny hair from Aurelie's ear and received a soft purr in return. "It's always been my greatest wish to spend my honeymoon with my not-yet husband and his mom, so this is a dream come true for me."

He grinned at this, and caught her eye. Her smile was something to behold. It only took him three steps to join her, and then he was clasping her in his arms. Kissing ensued, and when Mom opened the door a couple of minutes later, she wasn't greeted by happy faces, but the sight that met her eyes was enough to put a big smile on her own face. The kind of smile that said: I'm going to be a grandmother soon!

CHAPTER 39

Blake Carrington was in a good mood. He'd just received word that he was a shoo-in for the Gnome of the Year award, as he had expected, and that *Gnome & Gardens* would soon be in touch for the feature they were devoting to the winner of the competition. His picture would grace the cover of the magazine, so he would have to look his absolute best. Which meant a visit to Fido to have a haircut, and perhaps even a visit to the beauty parlor for a facial. He might be a man, but he didn't subscribe to the idea that only women were supposed to get facials and beauty treatments and such. In fact as he got older he was spending more and more time and money on his looks, and whenever someone told him he looked younger than his years, he felt gratified that it was all money well spent.

He picked up the paper again and continued reading about the stunning events that had taken place last night. Apparently there had been a big sting operation or some such malarkey, and the police had captured an actual pet-stealing gang who had kidnapped dozens of cats belonging to local pet owners with a view of extracting ransom money from these people. One of the kidnappers had been found dead in a water well located on the property where the pets had been held—the old Bailey farm on Helms Road that had been deserted and falling to pieces for years —in what looked like murder.

"A sordid business," Blake muttered under his breath. He glanced at his box of cigars, a bad habit but one he found hard to break. But as his hand traveled to the box to pick out a nice Havana, it suddenly halted in its tracks when his eye fell on the last paragraph of the article.

'According to police sources, the phone belonging to Gabriel Martinez, the man who was found at the bottom of the well, has yielded a vital clue to the identity of the mastermind behind the whole operation. An arrest is imminent.'

Blake's jaw dropped, and he broke out into a cold sweat. The Kingsley woman was the real deal, and her 'police sources' were her husband and her uncle, so if she wrote this, it must be true!

He was out of his chair in seconds, the paper fluttering to the floor. The only thought that occupied his mind was that he needed to get away. Good thing he had thought of every contingency after last night's disaster and had taken his precautions. His bags were packed and ready, and his passport was in perfect order. All he had to do was cross the border, and move to a non-extradition country. Brazil sounded like a good idea. It wasn't how he had imagined to spend his final years, but at least he wouldn't rot in prison.

And he had just picked up his suitcases and had descended the stairs when a sound at the door had him look up. The door flew open, and he suddenly found himself face to face with Detective Kingsley. For a moment he thought about doing a runner, but unfortunately his speed and agility were no match for Kingsley and his ilk.

So he put the suitcases down and gave the cop a weary smile. "Looks like you got me, Kingsley. So what mistake did I make?"

"You're under arrest, sir, for the murder of Gabriel Martinez, and conspiracy to kidnap dozens of cats, one dog and one infant."

"The infant was a mistake," said Blake. "I told Gabe to get rid of it immediately. I may be a lot of things but I'm not a baby snatcher, detective." The detective attached a pair of handcuffs to his wrists. "I really thought I had every angle covered," he told the cop. "So what did I do wrong? Your wife wrote in that paper of hers that you found something on Gabe's phone. So what was it? Some new forensic high-tech CSI stuff? They're always coming up with new ways to catch the bad guys, aren't they?"

"So you admit that you killed Gabriel Martinez?"

Blake shrugged. "He killed my boy, so it seemed appropriate."

"Martinez killed your son?"

"He did. Steven wanted to stop racing, but Gabe convinced him to give it one more shot. Turns out that Gabe had a lot of money riding on that race, and he couldn't afford to lose, which would have happened if Steven had pulled out, since he was the best. Gabe was supposed to be his friend, detective, but instead of looking out for him, he pushed him so he wouldn't pull out of that race. And we all know what happened next. My boy died, and for weeks Gabe pretended to be mourning his friend's death. Instead, he was mourning the loss of that wager, which by all accounts must have been substantial."

"Why wait ten years to get your revenge?"

"Because I didn't know! I only found out a couple of weeks ago, when I ran into another one of Steven's old friends, and he told me all about Gabe and the dubious role he played in my boy's death. And not only that, but the fact that a lot of people in this town knew all about what happened, but didn't bother to go after the people responsible. The organizers of that illegal street race, Gabe, the ones who set up those bets... I wanted to make them suffer the way I've suffered since Steven died." His expression turned grim. "You don't know what it's like to lose a child, detective. So I wanted people to get a taste of the same hell I've been living through for the past ten years. Losing a pet might not be the same thing as losing a child, but by all accounts it's as close as it gets."

"So you wanted the people of Hampton Cove to suffer the loss of their pets," said Kingsley, shaking his head. "But why cats, and not dogs? Though you did grab one dog, or was that by accident?"

"No, that was by design. You see, after Steven died, my shrink told me that one way to make my life livable again was to take up a hobby. And so I got into gnomes something big. And since my main competitors in this town are Tex Poole and Ted Trapper I wanted to nobble them first." He produced a weak smile. "Nothing like losing your beloved cat or dog to forget all about the upcoming Gnome of the Year contest, is there? Of course I didn't count on the fact that both Tex and Ted would be so obsessed with their gnomes that they wouldn't even notice that their pets had gone missing. So I had to resort to other means to sabotage their bid."

"And so you made Ted destroy Tex's prize gnome and vice versa," said Kingsley, nodding. "That was very clever of you."

Blake shrugged. "Just a little amateur psychology."

"You still haven't told me why you made Gabe pick cats and not dogs."

Blake frowned. "I guess it's because I quite like dogs myself, and I wouldn't want to see any harm come to them. Cats, on the other hand..." He made a face. "I've never cared for the species, to be honest. Oversized rats. Vile, vicious and vulgar. And Hampton Cove is full of them. It was about time someone did something to exterminate the pests. Wipe them from the face of the earth."

"My wife wouldn't agree," Kingsley said.

"Oh, I know. She loves those furballs, doesn't she?" He gave the detective a sly smile. "Too bad Gabe didn't get the chance to finish the job. But I knew you lot were getting closer to figuring out where he'd taken those pets, so I had to speed up my plan by getting rid of Gabe so he could see not only his reputation destroyed, but also his life."

"You're a real piece of work, aren't you, Carrington?" said Kingsley, and he took him by the shoulder and led him out of the house.

"So how did you figure it out?" asked Blake as he was taken to a squad car. But the detective didn't respond. Which is when Blake started to wonder if he'd been set up. It wouldn't surprise him one bit. Oh, well. At least he'd had his revenge. And as he was being driven away, he cast one final glance at his army of gnomes, standing at attention on the front lawn, saluting their master, and bidding him goodbye.

For now.

CHAPTER 40

"So how did you do it, Max?" asked Dooley. "How did you find the Terrific Master Word?"

"Who cares about the Master Soporific Word?" said Harriet. "What I want to know is how Max figured out that Blake Carrington was behind the petnappings and the murder."

We were on the porch swing, with the Poole family barbecue in full swing, and I glanced from my left to my right. To my left Dooley sat, and to my right Harriet and Brutus. All of them were staring at me, hoping for an answer, and even Odelia and Marge and Gran were listening intently, anxious to know how I had managed.

"Um, about the Soporific Word," I began.

"Nobody cares about that!" Brutus cried. "Tell us about the catnappings!"

"And let's not forget about the dognapping," said Rufus, who lay next to us on the porch, along with Fifi.

"Or the kidnapping," Fifi added.

"In short, everybody want to know about the naps," said Dooley.

"Nappings," Harriet corrected him. "It's all about the nappings."

"I don't think napping is actually a word," said Fifi.

"It is a word," said Dooley. "Napping is what we do. We nap at night, we nap during the day, we nap when we're tired and even when we're not tired. Napping is very important, you guys."

"Just let Max tell us about the kidnappings," Gran suggested. "After all, he hasn't told us how he figured it out."

"Well, it was actually something Gabe said when he was talking to his boss on the phone. He called him 'sir' all the time, and the way he spoke to him reminded me of something. It reminded me of the way a younger person addresses an older person they respect very much, like a teacher or a father figure. And so it got me wondering who this father figure could possibly be. So I asked Odelia to do a little digging into Gabe Martinez's background, and it turns out he was great friends with Steven Carrington, Blake's son who died in that street race."

"It didn't take me long to discover that Gabe was one of the organizers of that street race," Odelia continued. "And that he was heavily invested in the outcome of this particular race. He had borrowed money from a rich uncle and had promised him a good return on his investment. So when Steven threatened to pull out, Gabe leaned on him to change his mind. He simply couldn't afford for Steven not to race. All of Steven's friends I talked to said that if Gabe hadn't talked Steven into racing, he would still be alive today."

"Which got us wondering if Steven's dad could possibly be involved," I said. "And as luck would have it, one of Steven's friends remembered how he had bumped into Blake at a wedding a couple of weeks ago, and had told him about Gabe's role in his son's death. He says that Blake went completely pale, and had to sit down or else he would have fainted. Gabe's involvement and the gambling came as a great shock to him. He hadn't known, and had always treated Gabe like a son, knowing what a good friend of Steven he was. Over the years he had taken him under his wing, had given him a job at his company, and had even considered including him in his will."

"So when he heard about the terrible role Gabe had played," Odelia continued, "at first he was shocked, then swore revenge. And not just revenge on Gabe, but on everyone he felt had abandoned his son, which in his warped mind included all of Hampton Cove. Hence the petnappings, and Gabe's murder."

"So they were actually going to murder all of the pets?" asked Charlene. Uncle Alec's girlfriend was enjoying the cannelloni Chase had made. The latter was branching out from his signature dish of spaghetti bolognese into other Italian specialties and this one had been well received.

"That's right," Odelia confirmed. "Though I doubt whether that would have actually happened. Gabe was probably prepared to carry out Blake's command, but Johnny and Jerry had already made it clear they wanted no part in such a massacre, and would have fought him every step of the way."

"At least they did something right," said Marge.

"Anyone for a sausage!" Tex yelled. The doctor had managed to overcome his disappointment at ending second in the Gnome of the Year contest, and was back at the grill. "Sausages, anyone?"

Unfortunately Chase's cannelloni was so delicious that there were few takers for Tex's wares. Even the four of us had enjoyed some of that cannelloni sauce, which seemed to consist mainly of ricotta cheese and tomato sauce. Now

I'm not saying I'm big on tomatoes, but that ricotta wasn't half bad. Though when Tex started waving his sausage in the air, the four of us held up our tails. Cheese is all fine and dandy, but it will never be a match for a good piece of meat!

And so while the humans shunned the sausages, the good doctor found a receptive and appreciative audience in the six pets that lined his porch. It was a little scorched on the outside, but it was still pretty tasty.

"Such a terrible story," said Scarlett as she actually licked her plate and eyed Chase keenly, hoping for a refill. "How a man can be driven to do such horrible things."

"I think when Blake lost his son," said Marge, "he also lost part of his sanity. Especially when he discovered that Steven didn't have to die, but was compelled by one of his so-called friends to compete in that race."

"Steven still chose to get behind the wheel of that car," said Uncle Alec. "He could have said no, but instead he decided to compete, against his better judgment."

"At any rate, I think Max deserves a treat for figuring it out," said Marge.

"I'll give him some chocolate milk," said Gran, getting up.

"Gran, no!" said Odelia. "Never give chocolate to a cat! It's toxic for them!"

"Don't you think I know that?" said Gran with a smile. "But this is chocolate *milk,* and chocolate milk is fine."

Odelia gave her grandmother a look of concern. "Wait, have you been feeding the cats chocolate milk this past week?"

"Of course! And they love it. Don't you, sweeties?"

The four of us nodded. "It's very tasty," said Harriet.

"Really yummy," Brutus chimed in.

"It does taste nice," said Dooley.

"I like it," I said with a shrug.

"Gran, you can't do that!" Odelia said, looking thoroughly upset now. "Chocolate is bad for them. And chocolate milk is just as bad," she added when Gran opened her mouth to protest. "Even though diluted, it still contains chocolate, and chocolate contains theobromine, which is harmful to them. And besides, cow's milk isn't good for cats either. A lot of cats are lactose intolerant. It could give them stomach cramps and diarrhea."

Harriet gave me a look of concern. "Maybe that's why we couldn't sleep?"

"Of course you couldn't sleep!" said Odelia, and gave her grandmother a look of reproach. "Chocolate acts as a stimulant and increases your heart rate."

"Oh, Ma," said Marge, shaking her head.

The latter took it in stride, and muttered, "How the heck was I supposed to know that chocolate milk is just as bad as chocolate? What am I? Wikipedia?"

"So no more treats for the cats," said Odelia decidedly.

"That's all right," said Tex. "I already gave him a treat. A nice juicy sausage."

"Cooked up by you that's hardly what I'd consider a treat," said Marge, turning on her husband. She still hadn't forgiven him for taking a sledgehammer to their neighbor's prize gnome. Relations between the two men had been hostile ever since, even though Ted had done the exact same thing to Tex's main gnome.

"Does this mean you're the winner of the Gnome of the Year award?" asked Uncle Alec. "I mean, Blake will probably be disqualified after what he did, right?"

They all glanced at Tex, whose face was something to behold. At first he looked surprised, but then a big smile slid up his face. "You think?" he said.

"I think you stand a good chance," Uncle Alec

confirmed, giving Charlene a wink. The latter tried to hide a smile behind her napkin.

"Don't get the man's hopes up," she whispered.

"I'm not!" said the Chief. "It stands to reason, since Tex took second place."

"I wouldn't know," said Marge, just as coolly as before. "I'm not on the jury of that silly contest. But if I were, I'd disqualify not just Blake, but also Ted and Tex. They both behaved abominably."

"I just did what I had to do, honey," said Tex, spreading his arms. "A man has to fight for what he wants. It's the American way."

Marge turned a pair of cold eyes on her husband. "Cheating your way to victory is not the American way, Tex. Have you apologized to Ted, like I asked?"

"Not yet," said Tex, a mulish look stealing over him.

But Marge wasn't letting go. "So do it now. Or no more cannelloni for you. Isn't that right, Chase?"

"Um..." said Chase, who clearly didn't want to get involved in this particular domestic dispute.

"Ted is right there, Tex," said Marge, who had crossed her arms in front of her chest and stood regarding her husband with a distinct lack of affection. "So either apologize or you're sleeping on the couch tonight."

"But honey!"

"Indefinitely! Is that understood?"

"Yes, honey," said Tex meekly, and glanced over to the hedge that separated the two properties. And as we watched, a head popped up on the other side of the hedge, and we saw that Ted had appeared, with Marcie standing behind him, eyeing him with much the same expression as Marge was giving Tex.

"Now, Ted!" we could hear Marcie say.

"Yes, honey," Ted muttered weakly.

Both men approached the hedge, stared at one another for a moment, then Marge hissed, "Say you're sorry and shake the man's hand!"

"Just tell him already, Ted!" Marcie said. "Or you're sleeping on the couch!"

Tex and Ted exchanged a pained look, and I thought I detected a sort of understanding passing between the two men. An understanding that can only exist between two men finding themselves in a similar situation.

"I'm sorry, Ted," said Tex.

"I'm sorry, Tex," said Ted.

"And now say it as if you mean it!" Marge said.

"Well spoken, Marge!" said Marcie, and gave her neighbor a nod of appreciation, which Marge returned in kind.

Tex cleared his throat. "I'm sorry that I destroyed Robert Parker, Ted."

"And I'm sorry I took a great big whack at Norbert, Tex."

"I shouldn't have done it. It was wrong of me."

"Yeah, I guess I got tricked by Blake," said Ted.

"Wait, Blake told you to take out my Norbert?"

"He said it was the only way to win."

"He said the same thing to me!"

"And all the while he was looking out for number one," said Ted with a touch of bitterness. "Setting us up against each other."

"Did you know that he was the one who put those cameras up on our back fences? So he could spy on us and know what we were up to?"

"He kidnapped my dog, Tex, and he was going to kill him so I would pull out of the competition."

"He took my wife's cats," said Tex.

Ted shook his head as he leaned on the fence. "He's an evil person. Evil through and through."

"You can say that again. Now who in their right mind destroys another man's gnomes?"

"Exactly!"

They seemed to have forgotten that *they* were the kind of person who destroyed another man's gnomes. But at least they had buried the hatchet, united against the man who had tricked them into nobbling the competition.

Harriet and Brutus had jumped off the porch swing, and had disappeared into the rose bushes. Possibly to have a nap, or possibly not. Fifi and Rufus had also left the porch. A beautiful romance seemed to have sprung up between those two, and as everyone knows, young lovers—and even old ones—have better things to do than to spend time lounging on the porch with a couple of cats.

Meanwhile things had returned to normal in Hampton Cove. Dan had begged Odelia to come back to work. Apparently his great scheme of sourcing free copy from social media fans hadn't been the bonanza he was hoping for. He now claimed that the only reason he had consulted an employment lawyer was to hammer out a contract for the new contributors, making sure he owned their content. Also, rumor had it that several of the Gazette's loyal subscribers had staged an intervention, demanding he bring back the old format. Apparently Odelia's ties with the local 'forces of law and order' were no longer a concern.

"So how did you discover the Terrific Word, Max?" asked Dooley, who can be like a dog with a bone sometimes.

"Soporific Word," I corrected him automatically. I glanced left and right, making sure we were alone, then said, "It's just a word, Dooley. The first word that popped into my mind, actually."

Dooley gasped. "Did a word poop in your mind!"

"Not pooped, popped. Brutus was putting me under pressure, so I just gave him the first word I could think of. I'm not even sure this so-called Master Soporific Word exists, to be honest. It's probably just a myth."

"But then why does it work so well? We all fell asleep the moment we started using the word."

"Now that, my friend, is what they call the placebo effect."

"Play see what effect?"

"Placebo. The thing itself has no therapeutic quality whatsoever, but if you can get people to believe that it does, it works."

"But how?"

"Psychology," I said. "If you believe you will fall asleep when muttering some silly word to yourself, it just might happen."

"Huh," said my friend, as he thought about this for a moment. Then he smiled. "So you tricked us."

"I guess I did."

"You're a clever kitty, Max."

"Or a desperate kitty." When Brutus is leaning on you to deliver, you deliver, even if it's the first thing that pops into your head!

"Anyway, I don't believe you," said Dooley as he placed his head on his front paws. "This Terrific Word works too well for you to have made it up on the spot. I think you're simply being modest again, which is just like you, Max." And then he closed his eyes, and I could hear him muttering to himself, "Lollygags, lollygags, lollygagzzzzzz…" Soft snores told me my friend was sound asleep.

And as I settled down myself, preparatory to taking a nap, Flora fluttered into my field of vision.

"Hey, Flora," I said. "How is the racing going?"

"Absolutely great," she said. "In fact I just won a race this morning." She eyed me with a touch of concern. "I heard you were kidnapped? You and all the other cats in Hampton Cove?"

"We were," I confirmed. "But then we escaped, so all is well that ends well."

"That's good," she said, and fluttered down to take position next to me. "And now tell me all about this Soporific Word of yours. You might find this hard to believe, but I've been having trouble getting to sleep, too."

"Must be all of that nectar," I told her. "Maybe you should take a break from racing, Flora. Too much of a good thing might prove harmful, you know."

"I know, but I can't stop! I just keep winning and it's so much fun!"

"Okay, so the Master Soporific Word is... lollygag."

"Lollygag," Flora repeated quietly, then closed her eyes. It's hard to know when a butterfly actually goes to sleep, but since she stopped moving, and talking, my made-up soporific word had worked its magic yet again.

Or as Buddha used to say: there are many ways to catch a snake.

I guess I had found one way to catch a wink.

THE END

Thanks for reading! If you want to know when a new Nic Saint book comes out, sign up for Nic's mailing list: nicsaint.com/news

EXCERPT FROM PURRFECT YACHT (MAX 60)

Chapter One

I was basking in the sun—as one does—when the world decided to intrude upon my peace and quiet—as it does. As represented by Gran, the world perhaps had reason to interpose on my pleasant repose, since the news she had to impart was momentous—and I don't use this word lightly, as consequent events will bear out.

"It's happening!" she caroled as she came cantering into the backyard like a youngish foal. "It's actually happening!"

Dooley, alerted by this sudden emergence onto the scene of his human, looked startled. "Oh, no!" he cried. "What's happening!"

"I'm going!" Gran said, and performed a sort of NFL touchdown dance on the spot. "Or better yet: *we're* going."

"Going where, Gran?" I asked, patting my stricken friend on the back. Dooley looked not so much alarmed as downright spooked. All this talk about happenings and goings interrupting what must have been a refreshing nap was clearly having a deleterious effect on his sensitive soul.

"To the French Riviera, of course!" Gran cried.

Dooley and I shared a look of apprehension. Cats don't travel, everybody knows that. We're basically homebodies, and being dragged across oceans and continents to places one has never been might seem great fun to humans, but to us it sounds like something from a bad dream—or rather a nightmare!

"Why do we have to go to a French river era, Gran?" Dooley lamented. "And what is a river era?"

Gran stared at him. "Who said you're going anywhere?"

"But you said—"

"I said *we're* going to the French Riviera, not you."

"But—"

"Dick Bernstein and Rock Horowitz invited Scarlett and me to join them on Dick's yacht. His *yacht*!" she said, rubbing her hands with glee. "I've never been on an actual yacht before, so this is going to be a real treat!"

Somehow the news that his human was deserting him made Dooley feel even worse than the news that he might be traveling to France. "But Gran!" he cried. "You can't just leave us here all by ourselves!"

"You won't be all by yourselves," said Gran. "Marge will be here, and Odelia. In fact the whole family will be here. Except little old me," she added, tapping her chest proudly. "Since I'll be sunning and frolicking on a splendid yacht in the Mediterranean, having a ball!"

"Oh," said Dooley, who clearly didn't know whether to be happy that we were staying put, or sad that his human was leaving to go off on some crazy adventure. After all, Dick Bernstein and Rock Horowitz, Gran's friends from the senior center, are known for their eccentricity. So who knows when or even if Gran would ever return from this sojourn in one piece.

"When are you leaving?" I asked. "And how long will you be gone?"

"In two days," Gran said. "For a ten-day, all-inclusive exclusive sojourn on Dick's luxury yacht." She savored the words, rolling them around her tongue with relish. "This is all very much last notice, I know, but then the best things in life are like that: you just have to grab the chances life offers and be quick about it, too! In other words: you snooze, you lose!"

"But I like to snooze," Dooley lamented sadly.

"I think it sounds just great, Gran," I said, but somehow I couldn't hide my skepticism.

She fixed me with a baleful eye. Nobody likes a cat to rain on their parade, or any pet for that matter. "You don't approve, do you, Max?" she said. "Come on, spill. What's on your mind?"

"Nothing," I said. "It's just that..."

"It's just what?"

"Well, Dick Bernstein isn't exactly known as the most reliable person on the planet, and neither is Rock Horowitz. So are you sure you want to spend ten days on a yacht with those two guys?"

"Absolutely," she said with a big grin. "Too bad it's only ten days. When Dick told me about this I was hoping he'd say two months, or two years, or even twenty!"

"Twenty years!" Dooley said with a gasp. "But Gran!"

"Dick is such a dreamboat," said Gran wistfully.

"A dreamboat who owns a dream boat," I said with a yawn.

"His yacht is moored in the port of Nice, surrounded by plenty of other yachts, owned by celebrities and billionaires and whatnot. It's all very romantic—the stuff of Hollywood movies." She produced a slight squeal of excitement, making both Dooley and myself jump in surprise. "I better start packing! Or better yet, start shopping! I need an entire new wardrobe. Party dresses, bathing suits, lingerie..." She giggled like a schoolgirl as she clasped her hands together. "French Riviera, here I come!"

And without awaiting further comment from myself or Dooley, she was off at a trot, presumably on her way to borrowing her son-in-law's credit card so she could go on this pre-vacation shopping spree.

For a moment, neither Dooley or I spoke. Then he said: "I know I probably should be happy for Gran, Max, that she's been offered this unique opportunity, but for some reason I'm sad. And also worried."

"You're right to be worried," I said. "Gran being sprung upon an unsuspecting world like this is not a good idea. She'll probably get into all kinds of trouble over there."

"Maybe we should go with her, so we can keep an eye on her?" he suggested, but I could sense that his heart wasn't really in it.

"Let's just see what Marge has to say. And Alec, of course."

After all, if Gran wanted to go off on some French adventure, her son and daughter probably had some ideas about that. They might even call the whole thing off. And since Gran was currently living under Marge's roof, it wasn't inconceivable that Dick and Rock would have to find themselves another date.

And so it was that once the excitement of Gran's announcement had worn off, Dooley and I fell asleep once more. And a good thing, too, since we were both going to need our strength, considering the surprise life had in store for us next.

Chapter Two

Tex had been pruning the hedge when his mother-in-law came galloping out of the house and into Odelia's backyard. He heard her talking to her cats, and wondered what the big fuss was about. So when she returned, he had to suppress a strong urge to ask her what was going on. But knowing Vesta, whatever she had to say would merely serve to infuriate him on some level, so he kept his tongue, and pretended not to see her as he diligently focused on his hedge with an energy perhaps better reserved for a greater cause.

Long association with Marge's mother had taught him not to engage when she was on a rampage, and so when Marge approached him five minutes later, he could correctly claim that he had no idea what she was talking about when she said, "Did you hear the latest?"

"No, I did not," he said, and frankly he didn't want to know.

"She's going to France. On Dick Bernstein's yacht, of all places."

He frowned. Whatever he had been expecting, it definitely wasn't this. "Dick Bernstein owns a yacht?"

"It's the first I'm hearing of it. Apparently it belongs to his son, who runs an investment company. He uses the yacht to entertain potential clients, but since he's in China on a business trip, he's letting Dick have it for ten days. And since Dick doesn't want to spend that time alone on the yacht, he's invited his best friend Rock, and also my mother and Scarlett."

"How about that?" said Tex, and continued to snip away at the hedge. He knew better than to comment on his mother-in-law's plans. Vesta did what Vesta wanted to do, and no one had ever been able to stop her.

"You seem very relaxed about it?" said Marge, and she sounded a little peeved.

He shrugged. "She's old and wise enough. She doesn't need our permission. And it does sound like a great opportunity."

"I'm not so sure," said Marge. "I don't trust Dick, Tex. Remember when he told you to put mayonnaise on your head to cure your baldness?"

The good doctor grimaced. "Please don't remind me." It hadn't been his proudest moment. "Besides, maybe it helped? My hair seems to have grown back, hasn't it?"

"I told you then and I'm telling you now that your baldness was all in your imagination, honey," said Marge. "You were never going bald, so rubbing mayonnaise on your head didn't change a thing."

"I still think it worked," he insisted. Though it was true that Dick had confessed that he was simply pulling his leg when he had extolled the virtues of the so-called mayonnaise cure to him that time.

"I don't know, Tex," said Marge. "Maybe we should tell her not to go. You know what she's like. Before you know it she'll be up to her neck in trouble, and who do you think she'll call to bail her out?"

"I think it's fine," said Tex. "Scarlett will be there, and she's a sensible person."

"A sensible person! Scarlett is just as bad as my mother. Put the two of them together and you get a disaster. They seem to bring out the worst in each other." She had crossed her arms in front of her chest and was glaring at the house, where presumably Vesta was getting ready for her big trip. "She said she was going shopping. With the credit card you gave her, of course."

This time he did look up. "Shopping?" he asked in alarm.

"Said she needed a haircut, manicure, pedicure, and of course a new set of clothes. Bathing suits, dresses, *lingerie*.

I mean, what does she need lingerie for? She's seventy-five, for crying out loud, and she's been spending all of her life dressed in that same horrible tracksuit she likes so much."

Tex gulped. He knew just what would happen if Vesta went off on a shopping spree with his credit card. "C-c-can't you stop her?"

"Agent Provocateur," Marge said, shaking her head. "Can you imagine my mother in Agent Provocateur lingerie?"

"A-a-agent P-p-provocateur?!" Tex cried, dropping the hedge shears and almost hitting his big toe with the sharp end of the implement.

"Apparently," said Marge. "Though she might settle for Victoria's Secret." She threw up her hands. "I guess there isn't much we can do about it. Like you said, she's a grown woman and she doesn't need our permission."

"B-b-but we have to stop her!" said Tex, imagining the bill he would be saddled with if Vesta started raiding the Agent Provocateur or Victoria's Secret stores in a bid to look her best for Rock and Dick.

"Too late," said Marge, who seemed to devise a wicked pleasure in watching her husband squirm. "She left five minutes ago to pick up Scarlett. They're driving down to Manhattan. She said not to wait up for her. They'll have dinner in town. Might even catch a show or a movie to celebrate." She sighed. "Oh, well. At least we'll have some peace and quiet around here. I guess that's something to be grateful for." She studied her husband for a moment. "Remind me. What's the limit on that credit card you gave her?"

He goggled at her. "Why?"

"It might not be a bad idea to call the bank and get it lowered. Just for the foreseeable future. Say, for the next month or so?" And with these words, she turned on her heel and returned to the house.

It took a moment for his wife's words to register, but then Tex sprang into action. To take out his phone and dial his banker was but the work of a moment. Seconds later the call connected, and much to his satisfaction his banker only needed a few words to grasp this loyal customer's meaning.

"I know just what you're talking about, Doctor Poole," said Martin Schofield. "Like you, I have a mother-in-law. And just like you, she's the bane of my existence. So let's get that credit lowered, shall we?"

"How long is this going to take?" asked Tex nervously.

"Not long," Martin assured him with typical breeziness.

"It's just that she already left for Manhattan," he said. "She's going for a full makeover. Hair, nails, clothes—the works. She said she wants to buy..." He gulped, his Adam's apple bopping up and down. "She wants to buy..." He squeezed his eyes shut and practically whispered, "Agent Provocateur lingerie."

"That bad, huh?" said Martin good-naturedly. "Looks like we've got ourselves a genuine emergency on our hands. Defcon One, would you say?"

"Definitely Defcon One," said Tex, happy to get the banker's full cooperation.

"Us sons-in-law have to stick together, Tex," said Martin gravely. "In fact we should probably start a club. Join forces, if you know what I mean. We could call it the son-in-law survivors club." Tex heard some tapping of fingers on keys, and moments later the banker quoted a number. "What do you think? Higher? Lower?"

"Lower," said Tex in a low voice. "Much, *much* lower."

Chapter Three

Emily King had been counting the days until she could finally leave and be with her fiancé. Harry had already left last week, but she couldn't leave her colleagues at Fat-Less in the lurch, so she had decided to keep working until the final day before her departure for the South of France. The Audrey was awaiting her arrival, and so was Harry, and if what he said was to be believed, also his parents. Frankly she had her doubts about that, since Steven and Amanda Griffiths hadn't exactly seemed overly pleased when Harry had introduced her. And when he told them that Emily wasn't merely his girlfriend but that he had actually proposed to her, the look on Amanda's face spoke volumes. The woman clearly wasn't in agreement with her son's choice for a future spouse, and Emily imagined harsh words had been spoken the moment she had left the Griffiths parental mansion.

Harry hadn't mentioned anything about an argument, but then he always did go out of his way to protect her. When Harry had joined her Zumba class last year, she had immediately noticed not only his athleticism but also his outrageously good looks. But since she was a professional she hadn't let that affect the way she treated him—giving him the exact same level of attention she gave all of her students. No more, no less. But the attraction had been unmistakable, and reciprocal, for it hadn't taken Harry long to invite her for a drink.

She had wavered for a while, since she had a strict rule about not mixing her professional life with her personal. But a girl can only resist for so long, and when he showed up one morning with a small troupe of friends, performing an impromptu flash mob style dance routine, she had relented. One date had led to another, and it was over the course of dinner that he had announced that he was falling for her. She couldn't deny that the feeling was mutual, and soon they had become inseparable.

Which is when he had carefully broached the subject of his family. And their wealth. For the Griffiths were well off. Like, really well off. Their mansion, located on the outskirts of Hampton Cove, had to be seen to be believed, and if she was overwhelmed, she tried not to show it. Clearly the scornful smile on Amanda's face had indicated she had failed in that particular endeavor. Then again, how could she not be impressed? Her own mom had worked all her life as a cleaner, and her dad was a car mechanic, so the King family wasn't exactly swimming in money. But even though she wanted to assure Harry's folks that she wasn't dating him for his money, somehow she knew they wouldn't believe her. Somehow the word gold digger had been dropped into the conversation at some point, even though later on Emily couldn't remember the context, or even if the reference was aimed at her. Probably not, since Amanda was too subtle for that. Or too shrewd. But the meaning was clear, and the visit had left a bad taste in her mouth.

So when Harry had invited her to join the family on their annual vacation in the South of France, she'd had her doubts. Did she really want to spend two weeks in close quarters with these people? Did they even want her there? Harry had assured her that his mother had personally invited her. That she wanted to get to know her future daughter-in-law. And so eventually she had caved. In fact it was her own mother who had convinced her to accept the invitation.

"I'm sure that once Amanda Griffiths gets to know you, she'll learn to love you, just like everyone who knows you does," said Mom. It had been a touching moment, and when her dad had added that if the Griffiths gave her any trouble he'd fix them good—whatever that meant—she had relented.

What was the worst that could happen? Some mean-spirited comments and dirty looks? She could live with that. If it meant spending two weeks with Harry on a majestic yacht moored in the port of Saint-Tropez and enjoying a sun-soaked holiday, she'd be crazy to say no. So she said yes—wholeheartedly yes!

But that was before the first message arrived. And the picture.

She stared at her phone, still not fully understanding what she was looking at, exactly. She recognized the picture, of course she did. But what she failed to grasp was the message that accompanied it.

'Better think again!'

Think again? Think about what?

Whoever had sent the picture must have realized the vagueness of the message, for the second text she received shortly after the first one read: 'Break up with Harry, or I send these pictures to the Griffiths!'

Now that was much clearer. But also a lot more terrifying!

She studied the picture. It had been taken by her ex-boyfriend, the guy she'd been dating when she met Harry. It had been one of those on-and-off affairs, though more off than on, to be honest. And during one of their on episodes, he had asked her to pose for him, which she had happily done, since she was proud of her figure, honed through years of hard work in the gym, and didn't mind showing it off.

Now that she saw the snap again, though, she could see the trouble she was in. It wasn't all that risqué. There wasn't even a lot to see that would bring a blush of shame to the cheek of modesty. But to Amanda Griffiths it would confirm the notion that Emily simply wasn't the right choice for her precious son.

And then there was the clause, of course.

The infamous Griffiths Clause!

Now there lay the rub.

ABOUT NIC

Nic has a background in political science and before being struck by the writing bug worked odd jobs around the world (including but not limited to massage therapist in Mexico, gardener in Italy, restaurant manager in India, and Berlitz teacher in Belgium).

When he's not writing he enjoys curling up with a good (comic) book, watching British crime dramas, French comedies or Nancy Meyers movies, sampling pastry (apple cake!), pasta and chocolate (preferably the dark variety), twisting himself into a pretzel doing morning yoga, going for a run, and spoiling his big red tomcat Tommy.

He lives with his wife (and aforementioned cat) in a small village smack dab in the middle of absolutely nowhere and is probably writing his next 'Mysteries of Max' book right now.

www.nicsaint.com

ALSO BY NIC SAINT

The Mysteries of Max

Purrfect Murder

Purrfectly Deadly

Purrfect Revenge

Purrfect Heat

Purrfect Crime

Purrfect Rivalry

Purrfect Peril

Purrfect Secret

Purrfect Alibi

Purrfect Obsession

Purrfect Betrayal

Purrfectly Clueless

Purrfectly Royal

Purrfect Cut

Purrfect Trap

Purrfectly Hidden

Purrfect Kill

Purrfect Boy Toy

Purrfectly Dogged

Purrfectly Dead

Purrfect Saint

Purrfect Advice

Purrfect Passion

A Purrfect Gnomeful

Purrfect Cover

Purrfect Patsy

Purrfect Son

Purrfect Fool

Purrfect Fitness

Purrfect Setup

Purrfect Sidekick

Purrfect Deceit

Purrfect Ruse

Purrfect Swing

Purrfect Cruise

Purrfect Harmony

Purrfect Sparkle

Purrfect Cure

Purrfect Cheat

Purrfect Catch

Purrfect Design

Purrfect Life

Purrfect Thief

Purrfect Crust

Purrfect Bachelor

Purrfect Double

Purrfect Date

Purrfect Hit

Purrfect Baby

Purrfect Mess

Purrfect Paris

Purrfect Model

Purrfect Slug

Purrfect Match

Purrfect Game

Purrfect Bouquet

Purrfect Home

Purrfectly Slim

Purrfect Nap

The Mysteries of Max Collections

Collection 1 (Books 1-3)

Collection 2 (Books 4-6)

Collection 3 (Books 7-9)

Collection 4 (Books 10-12)

Collection 5 (Books 13-15)

Collection 6 (Books 16-18)

Collection 7 (Books 19-21)

Collection 8 (Books 22-24)

Collection 9 (Books 25-27)

Collection 10 (Books 28-30)

Collection 11 (Books 31-33)

Collection 12 (Books 34-36)

Collection 13 (Books 37-39)

Collection 14 (Books 40-42)

Collection 15 (Books 43-45)

Collection 16 (Books 46-48)

Collection 17 (Books 49-51)

Collection 18 (Books 52-54)

Collection 19 (Books 55-57)

The Mysteries of Max Big Collections

Big Collection 1 (Books 1-10)

Big Collection 2 (Books 11-20)

The Mysteries of Max Short Stories

Collection 1 (Stories 1-3)

Collection 2 (Stories 4-7)

Nora Steel

Murder Retreat

The Kellys

Murder Motel

Death in Suburbia

Emily Stone

Murder at the Art Class

Washington & Jefferson

First Shot

Alice Whitehouse

Spooky Times

Spooky Trills

Spooky End

Spooky Spells

Ghosts of London

Between a Ghost and a Spooky Place

Public Ghost Number One

Ghost Save the Queen

Box Set 1 (Books 1-3)

A Tale of Two Harrys

Ghost of Girlband Past

Ghostlier Things

Charleneland

Deadly Ride

Final Ride

Neighborhood Witch Committee

Witchy Start

Witchy Worries

Witchy Wishes

Saffron Diffley

Crime and Retribution

Vice and Verdict

Felonies and Penalties (Saffron Diffley Short 1)

The B-Team

Once Upon a Spy

Tate-à-Tate

Enemy of the Tates

Ghosts vs. Spies

The Ghost Who Came in from the Cold

Witchy Fingers

Witchy Trouble

Witchy Hexations

Witchy Possessions

Witchy Riches

Box Set 1 (Books 1-4)

The Mysteries of Bell & Whitehouse

One Spoonful of Trouble

Two Scoops of Murder

Three Shots of Disaster

Box Set 1 (Books 1-3)

A Twist of Wraith

A Touch of Ghost

A Clash of Spooks

Box Set 2 (Books 4-6)

The Stuffing of Nightmares

A Breath of Dead Air

An Act of Hodd

Box Set 3 (Books 7-9)

A Game of Dons

Standalone Novels

When in Bruges

The Whiskered Spy

ThrillFix

Homejacking

The Eighth Billionaire

The Wrong Woman

CPSIA information can be obtained
at www.ICGtesting.com
Printed in the USA
LVHW092054220323
742311LV00016B/1505

9 789464 446647